THE TRUEST SENSE

A Collection of Horrors

Laura Keating

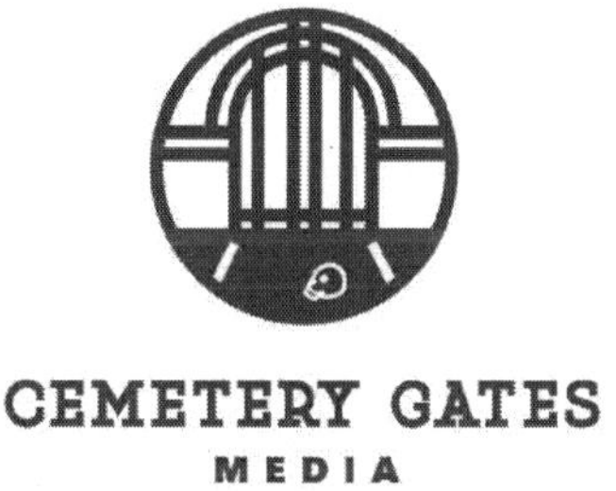

The Truest Sense
Published by Cemetery Gates Media
Binghamton, New York

ISBN: 9798322757962

For more information about this book and other Cemetery Gates Media publications, visit us at:

cemeterygatesmedia.com
twitter.com/cemeterygatesm
instagram.com/cemeterygatesm

Cover Art and Design: Chad Wehrle

"Laura Keating's exploration of her own horror roots finds transcendence in *The Truest Sense*. From gleeful genre romps and frightening fabulism to sublime excursions along the borderlands of the weird, Keating carves a path to horror's hidden heart."

—Gordon B. White, finalist for the
Shirley Jackson Award

"Atmospheric, gorgeously written and imaginative as all hell. What a basket full of treats this collection is."

—Gemma Amor, Bram Stoker Award nominated
author of *Dear Laura*

"*The Truest Sense* is a masterfully executed collection that cuts to the quick. Keating proves two things with her latest book: she's a must-read name in the genre and she's absolutely here to stay."

—Caitlin Marceau, award-winning author of
This is Where We Talk Things Out

REPRINTS:

"The Kissing Gate" first published in PerVisions Magazine, 2017.

"We Are Giants" first published in *Giants and Ogres: Fairy Tale Villains Reimagined*, CBAY books, 2017.

"Good Time in the Bad Lands" first published in *Worst Laid Plans: An Anthology of Vacation Horror*, Grindhouse Press, 2020.

"Lakebottom Charlie" first published in *Campfire Macabre Vol. II,* Cemetery Gates Media, 2023.

CONTENTS

To Johnny

FOREWORD

The title of this book was inspired by a tweet wherein someone (I believe it was Tenebrous Press editor Alex Woodroe, but I could be misremembering) said they had been told that their story was not horror in "the truest sense." That made me laugh, because at the end of the day (at least my day) horror is *the* Truest Sense, the sense we've all known since we were pulled howling into the world, wondering what the hell just happened and where we are now.

Horror is a genre of questions, inviting you to pluck just enough slime out of the unknown to get a good, nasty look at it. Did you ever dive down to the bottom of a lake as a kid (or last week, who am I to judge?) and grab a fistful of stinking mud off the bottom, just to see what was down there? Just to send a shiver down your spine? And as you hold it up, black muck oozing between your fingers, small rocks grating together, you wonder if maybe you can feel something wriggling inside, maybe something that bites? You don't know, but that *maybe* that *sense* is the important thing as you send it back, screaming (and laughing, just a little) and that's a good enough truth even if it's not quite an answer.

In this collection, you'll find doomed explorers, haunted geography, witches, demons, and hellish home renovations. Most of it is set within the boundaries of East Coast Canada—or at least some twisted version of it—and I hope I don't put tourism in the Maritimes too far back. Most of these stories have never been published before; black muck getting its first-ever taste of fresh air.

I began compiling this collection in the winter of 2023 in Montreal and ended in a small fishing town in Nova Scotia on a hot summer day later the same year. I thought that I'd submit the whole manuscript early, instead it was at the bottom of the deadline—which is just life, I guess, sneaking up on you like a guy in a rubber mask. While I was busy packing up one huge chapter of my life, these stories waited patiently and did not blink. But I made it out, which means I guess means I get to go on to the sequel. And like your favourite masked killer, it was comforting to see these stories all again when I finally had a chance to sit and put them in some semblance of order, to remember where I was when I wrote them. Your senses stay with you, are a part of you, even when everything else changes. Despite my labors and overthinking of order, I invite you to read these stories in any order you like, whatever makes sense.

Laura,
July 2023, South Shore NS.

FINAL NOTES ON THE FAILED EXPEDITION TO THE SIXTH THEATRE

Theatre One

Northeast entrance, one meter in diameter; passage twenty meters. Surveyors required to crawl. Graffiti of large star and eye in red acrylic paint observed at fourth meter unrelated to expedition. Passage opens into primary chamber, hereafter known as Theatre One. Large ursine tracks observed across the floor, beginning at the eastern quadrant and terminating down the westward tunnel, disappearing into the dark. The tracks on the soft clay floor are detailed, so fresh in appearance they might have been made the day before. They are estimated to be approximately twenty-thousand-years old.

This is only the first of the many mysteries of the Lancaster Theatre Caves. *Ursus spelaeus* are thought to have gone extinct twenty-*five*-thousand years ago. No species of this size has ever been recorded outside of Europe and Asia. Furthermore, all geological evidence suggests that this region of Atlantic Canada was—at that time these tracks would have been made—covered by the great Laurentide Ice Sheet, which would not recede until 11, 000 BCE.

While the presence of the tracks goes against several previously understood scientific estimates, their preservation is extraordinary. A rockslide sealed the caves around the time of the last Ice Age.

For the public's safety, since the loss of the Gorska-Dwyer expedition, they have been sealed once again.

Theatre One, sometimes referred to as The Lobby, is adorned with prehistoric scenes: feeding ruminants, grasslands, a woolly mammoth (another mystery, the species is not thought to have had ranged to this portion of the globe during the Pleistocene Epoch), a band of both hunters and gatherers, and the rising sun.

Each charcoal and ochre image was painted with a confident hand and detailed further with fine chisel lines, giving the antelope three heads, the mammoths six trunks, the humans innumerable arms. Initially thought to be fanciful depictions, perhaps even a prehistoric mythology, the gentle swing of a lantern coaxes the ancient interplay of light, line, and shadow back to life. After twenty millennia dormant, the theatre wakes.

Heads lift and warily turn; great rolling muscle flex, powerful trunks sway; men and women raise their arms to a great revolving eye or lie prostrate before its glare. Not recorded on celluloid but on stone, these are the first known moving pictures, and the Stone Age people who gathered to watch them, the first theatre-going audiences. The power of these images is undeniable, yet they are the mere previews of the chambers to come.

With the caves now sealed, in place of audience access we have the exploration notes, imaging scans, and collected artifacts of earlier expeditions—as well as the scant film footage taken by Dr. Maria Gorska's geological survey team and by Dr. Hamilton Dwyer's paleontological team. Like the cave paintings themselves, the footage, equipment, cameras, and single body recovered by the rescue crew sent to retrieve the Gorska-Dwyer expedition after they failed to emerge offer few answers and leave only tantalizing clues.

No exterior light penetrates the caves. Only a limited number of LED headlamps were permitted to the expedition—a precaution taken to reduce the risk of additional heat and moisture in the delicate environment. The six scientists were as evenly divided in their number as they were on their feelings about this safeguard. For Dr. Gorska and her team of three, this made perfect sense; damage had already been done to the Lascaux caves in France, when moisture from the warm lips of the many visitors coupled with the heat of the spotlights allowed mold to flourish in the once pristine conditions. Dr. Dwyer, however, was bitterly disappointed. In one of his final emails to his colleague at the University of Dalhousie, he remarked: *The work was done by fire and can only be brought to life by the same; the cold eye of a diode steals the essence away.*

Theatre Two

Southwest entrance. Natural formation. The walls are smooth, the curves and sharp angles still retaining the shape of the underground river which dried a millennia before the artists and builders of the Theatre Caves arrived. At the western-most corner of the ceiling, several small indentations, roughly square, set at approximately twenty-three-degree angles. The prevailing theory is that they provided a light source for Theatre Two. The placement of the bored indents suggests that the Stone Age architects had a working knowledge of astronomy, the solar year, and the Metonic Cycle. Ground to surface scans have revealed that the indentations connect to now filled shafts which were in perfect alignment for the setting sun of the Winter and Summer Solstices.

Artificial light was applied to recreate the conditions. Dr. Dwyer filmed the results.

On the eastern wall, the sun begins to climb. Long grasses sway and rolling hills rise and fall like a beating heart on the horizon. As the chiseled sun stretches, creatures stir and wake: shaggy bulls, horses, dogs. None should exist here, not at the time of carving. Yet they step from out from an impossible past, their many legs carrying them the length of the cave wall. Man rises from the tall grass, not to hunt but to walk alongside the animals. Together the peaceful procession, a swirl of life from all walks and innumerable ages, advances deeper into the caves, single-minded and drawn towards a lone beckoning figure.

The light is lifted from the walls, and the painted forms freeze in place once more. The expedition shares amazed smiles. One can only imagine what they felt in that moment, the first live audience in millennia. They cannot tell us.

Theatre Three

Natural formation with man-made augmentation. A small platform carved into stone at north quadrant, near the entrance, with a hollowed and smoothed backing. In the center of the chamber, a stalagmite cut in half with the surface ground smooth. Atop this pedestal, a bone flute (see: Appendix B) was discovered by an earlier expedition. A digital 3D model was rendered and printed. The model was brought back to the cave for this study. Radiocarbon dating of the original flute places its age at roughly twenty-two thousand years old. Further analysis concluded the bone was human, possible the tibia or fibula of an adolescent male.

Unlike any other known cave art, the subjects of this room are not only predominantly humanoid but display detailed features. No stick figures, these are comprehensive portraits in ancient charcoal: a man carrying a small child, a group of women kneeling at a stream, a trio of youths building a fire. Scenes of domestic life from a lost era, a treasure-trove for the field of paleoanthropology. Dr. Dwyer's footage yet again provides us with a glimpse into this lost world.

In the moving portraits lit by the LED lights, friends embrace, heads are tipped back in laughter, a cup of water is enjoyed. Their movements are small and resolute, like a hologram card tipped back and forth to reveal the trick image.

The cave around Dr. Gorska is black, the stalagmites at her sides shiver in the restless glow of the cameraman's spotlight. She steps back and adjusts her headlamp so it is not blinding the lens. Her excitement is evident.

Dr. Gorska makes a brief statement about the striations in the rock, the collisions of continents in this geopark—but she is interrupted by a low, sighing whistle. The cave is obscured as the camera moves around. Dr. Dwyer has instructed one of his students to stand on the platform and there they play a single, sustained note on the replica flute. Beside him, Dr. Dwyer holds a real lit candle. Dr. Gorska is horrified.

"Blow that out."

"Turn off the lights," Dr. Dwyer says.

There is a moment of heated argument.

"Fire is the natural thing here," Dwyer argues. Perhaps to hasten the end of the experience, Dr. Gorska abruptly turns to the cameraman and makes an annoyed gesture. The camera tips, buttons are fumbled, the sound buffeted, and the film goes black.

It takes a few seconds for the camera to adjust to the near-dark. When focus returns by the light of the candle, the chamber is transformed.

The low note of the flute fills the space. Candle aloft, Dr. Dwyer slowly walks the length of the Theatre, from back to entrance. By the warm flame, limbs appear to twitch, to move, and portraits change. Walking backwards towards the entrance, embraces turn from friendly to sensual to cruel; the drinking cup is revealed to be the upended top of a skull, it overflows with dark colours; the heads of the gathered women slowly turn, laughs reverse, their eyes narrow as if alerted to the presence of the interlopers. One woman raises her hand. Her face splits into a wide, sharp, smile and, beckoning, she steps backwards into the next chamber, disappearing into the shadows.

Dr. Dwyer turns and walks from entrance to backend. Walking with candle in this way, the scenes at play are bucolic once more. The expedition, Gorska included, is in tears. The results are, in short, outstanding. Dr. Dwyer's bold experiment—which while not supported by the University—and its outcome will be studied with great admiration and interest in his absence.

Assurances have been made to the Lancaster Falls Police that there was no one else in the caves at the time of this expedition. Before becoming permanently sealed to the public, the entrance to the caves was locked with a specially fitted door. The area is remote and not easily accessible; exact coordinates are required to orienteer to the site. But so vivid is the aspect and appearance of the smiling woman, her very ancient reality was called into question. We assert here, formally, that she is not real but a stirring testament to the skill of the Stone Age artisans who brought her to life and captured her so elegantly (and fortunately) on film by the lost Gorska-Dwyer team.

The original film file remains with the Lancaster Falls police department. A digital copy has been provided for this notation.

Theatre Four

Manmade cavern. Forty meters by seventy meters, roughly pear shaped. The chisel work is exact and evenly spaced. The walls—once painted red and combined with the chisel work—gives the room the appearance of fibrous tissue, like the interior of a vital organ. A large cave bear skeleton was discovered in center of the room (see: Referent H) ritualistically posed (see: Appendix E) with the skull placed between the legs in a uroboros/birthing position. Knife marks on the bones suggest the animal was skinned down to the bone, perhaps while alive. Mummified remains of fur belonging to same animal discovered along eastern wall.

Images on eastern wall: winter and summer skies. Prominent indentations (as noted in earlier chamber) corresponding with winter constellations (specifically Auriga, Orion and Taurus) feature at northern length. Prominent indentations corresponding with summer constellations (Cygnus, Ursa Major and Minor, Lyra) feature at southern length. Ritualistic display of bear theorized to be part of Solstice ritual sacrifice.

The illusion of motion is not unique to the Lancaster Theatre Caves. Similar images and similar theories have been proposed about both Lascaux and the Chauvet caves of France. Neither are the Lancaster cave's images the oldest—that honor goes to Leang Tedongnge cave in a secluded valley on the island of Sulawesi, Indonesia. What makes the Theater Caves astounding is the mesmerizing detail, the subject matter, and the mysteries they invoke, the questions they invite.

The woman observed in Dr. Dwyer's film entering from Theatre Three is now present throughout Theatre Four. In Theatre Three, she is seen once in a group image. In Theatre Four, she is a solitary figure: here smiling (distantly) over a group of children, there urging plants to grow, arms spread in welcome. She may represent a forgotten fertility or harvest deity (affectionately known now to those in the field as the Matron).

One researcher, Dr. William Lawson—from the earlier survey team, Expedition Two—noted that a great deal of difference could be observed in the Matron's appearance based whether you were coming or going into the chamber. He reported that upon arrival to the Fourth Theatre, under the bright, static LED floodlights, the Matron is the subject of comforting paintings. But upon exiting, one by one, the team's headlights growing dimmer, her aspect changed, arms moving not in welcome but reaching out, almost grasping, for the backs of the retreating expedition. Dr. Lawson did not make a second trip to the caves and no one else ever noted such, but something similar appears on one of the cameras of Dr. Gorska's team. It is for posterity that we record only the facts of the following.

In the final film found, Drs. Gorska and Dwyer are in heated argument. Leadership has broken down. It appears they cannot find the tunnel back, only the one leading to the next chamber. The unknown cameraman, likely of Gorska's team, joins her in accusing Dwyer of reckless behaviour, insist that they need to return to get help. The student who played the replica flute in Theatre Three is briefly appears on screen. Sitting on the dirt floor, he is naked from the waist down and badly injured by apparent self-mutilation. He is in a state of ecstasy.

Dr. Dwyer attempts to seize the camera and prevent further recording, blurring and shaking the scene. There are sudden, panicked calls from the others and the camera pans across the back legs of the injured student as he crawls into the small tunnel towards Theatre Five.

It is here, due to the haste of the camera work and the motion of the teams' headlights, that by fortunate accident we may observe the phenomenon recounted by Expedition Two.

The full team tries to pull the injured student back, but his legs are slick with blood. The circle of headlights about the carved walls gives the sudden, incredible effect of multiple thin arms reaching, all at once, like the legs of a trap-spider, from the narrow tunnel. The expedition jumps backwards from the illusions, the light play is broken, and the student disappears down the tunnel. Dr. Gorska takes a final, stunned look into the lens and the camera is abruptly turned off.

Air quality tests were taken as part of the later recue effort and no traces of any substance which might have produced any adverse effects were found. All behaviours are speculated to be purely psychological in nature and not the result of negligence on the part of the University.

Chair's Note: As of writing, Theatres Four and Five remain an active crime scene. Cave Bear bone and fur piles have been contaminated by presence of human tissues. Any and all future soil sample collection potentially contaminated.

Theatre Five

Natural formation. Two by three meters, connected to Theatre Four by a small umbilicus. Surveyors and rescue team required to crawl, belly to floor. Immediately faced with a graphic birth scene. A seated female figure depicted naked, legs spread, roots/ branches spring from her vagina. Her face is a tree, or some other accumulation of limbs. Unclear if she is meant to represent the maternal female figure of Theatre Four. In her left hand, she holds the sun, in her right hand, a black sphere. All images in the caves are drawn to this point. By a single headlight, the branches appear to writhe and grow. The significance of this image to the people who carved it can only be projected upon. Possible representation of day and night, or of spiritual rebirth.

Below this tableau, the body of the student, Edwin Morgan, was discovered by the rescue team. We will omit details of the nature of his remains out of respect for his family. The following inscription, carved by the student himself with a small stone implement, was discovered on the wall above the small chamber entrance: "Death is birth."

The whereabouts of the five other members of the Gorska-Dwyer Expedition remains unknown and under investigation.

Theatre Six

Full specifications not available. Undiscovered until the recovery efforts made to retrieve Dr. Gorska, Dr. Dwyer, and their teams. No earlier expedition ever reported a sixth chamber or any channels leading to a sixth room. As such, no detailed survey has been conducted. What we have is the brief information relayed from the Search and Rescue report.

Initial Notes from Search and Rescue: [sic] Small hole at the back of "Theatre Five roughly one-inch in diameter. Cold wind can be felt behind it, use of flashlights revealed large unexplored cavern. Rescue observed human voices emanating from small hole, initially thought to be screaming, but more likely wind through tunnels. No evidence of cave-in but there remains the possibility an entrance to "Theatre Six" closed behind the Gorska-Dwyer Expedition. Search for such a former entrance ongoing. Location of five missing scientists: inconclusive. [sic]

Ground-penetrating scans from the surface reveal nothing, no detectable caverns. Yet human observation concludes something is further back, that there is a "Sixth Theatre" overlooked by all previous expeditions. It is an incredibly exciting development. One can only hope that access to the Theatre Caves will soon be restored so that a careful and renewed investigation can commence. Perhaps by Dr. Dwyer's methods, we might recreate even more astounding results and more fully bring this forgotten past back to life.

THE KISSING GATE

When I was four, I saw two boys go into the woods behind our house. They did not come out again. They were big boys, maybe ten or eleven. The bigger of the two wanted to go through the iron kissing gate there and take the overgrown path into the pine woods. He'd met a queen, he said, a real queen, with golden hair and starry eyes, and she was waiting. The smaller boy said there was no such thing as queens anymore, but he went all the same.

I sat still, watching from a cedar hedge. I'd been told never to walk anywhere alone, but especially the woods. The woods were dangerous, my father said. There used to be an old farm back down that path, and old farmers always left junk around: rusted tin cans, barbed wire, old tools. And there were natural dangers too: rocks to trip on, or holes to break a leg in. And you never knew who you might meet in the woods.

"Who?" I asked. Someone bad who might want to take you away, he said. "Why?" Just away, my father said.

I told my parents about the boys when they were reported missing on the evening news two nights later. I recognized the smaller boy's sweater: green with a blue rocket on it. A search team was assembled and neighbours, police officers, and dogs arrived at our home. One group took the path between the trees, the others spread out through the underbrush, leaving trails in the long grass like spreading fingers. My mother made sandwiches; I helped to make lemonade. I felt so grown-up.

On the second day, a nice police officer asked me to describe, again, what the boys had been wearing. The next day after that a reporter asked me if I had seen anyone else, maybe a man go into the woods with the boys. I said no, but maybe they found the queen. My father came out of the house and took me inside. He told me to watch cartoons. This made me happy. Usually, I wasn't allowed to watch television when it was sunny outside. Many of the people who wanted to help had children of their own and they brought them to our house. That is how I met Diane.

We were the same height and we even looked a little bit the same, although her hair was as blonde and as fine as corn silk, and mine was as dark as turned earth. We played Secret Princesses; all games were named back then. On the incomplete back patio, crawling between the unfinished slats, twirling around the square-edged posts, we breathlessly instructed one another on the rules as we went: "Okay, now pretend . . . now pretend, okay?" My mom gave us ice-creams. They were the same flavour, but Diane invited me to try hers, and I did. We giggled when I held her hand. I hoped that the boys were never found; I hoped they would look for them forever.

After a few weeks, the search party was called off. They had found nothing beyond the kissing gate but an old sneaker. It was the right size, but far too old and broken down to belong to one of the boys. I said it looked right, a bright green high-top. No one said so, but I could tell that everyone doubted that I had really seen anything at all, that I must have thought I was helping. I earned the reputation for having a vivid imagination—which I supposed was at least a nice way to be called a liar.

"Do you ever wonder about the boys?" I asked Diane, several years later. We sat on my rusted, red swing-set, our shoes scuffing the dry dirt under the seats, raising small brown clouds.

"What boys?" she said.

The swing set was too small for us now, and it *cha-chung*ed whenever I swung. Mom said I would break my neck on it, and dad was going to take it down that evening. He didn't though, he forgot. It collapsed two weeks later when I was on it. I ended up with stitches. I still have the scar.

"The missing boys," I said, watching the little gate at the bottom of the yard. I reached up and pulled the tight chains of my swing together, spinning myself a little.

"No," Diane said. "I don't remember."

I said, "I wonder if they're dead," and I pulled on one of her chains, pulling her closer to me. "Still back there. Little skeletons now." Our seats touched.

Diane jumped up. Her empty swing twitched uselessly from my hand, like an organ not yet aware it's been cut out. I felt bad. I let it drop. It squeaked as it swung stiffly.

"Don't be weird," she told me.

I felt angry. "You forgot them anyway."

Her cheeks were flushed. She licked her lips with just the tip of her tongue. "Just don't be weird," she said.

***

There is kindness in fiction. I started making my own stories. Even if it is a sad story, everyone is satisfied by the end. Because it *does* end. I filled my tales with characters who always solved the riddles, and nothing was ever forgotten. If someone is hurt or something goes wrong in a story, any story, you just have to go back to the beginning and there they are, safe and sound.

***

In middle school, I would invite Diane over to read magazines, or to do homework. She didn't invite me over as much, but she would still show up when I called. We were mostly good, but to this day I cannot stomach the smell of anise. Diane and I had bought a plastic pint of Pernod from some older girls, overpaying, I know now, by a considerable amount. They said it was absinth, and we thought we were being dangerous; we wanted to see green faeries.

I do not remember ever seeing the older girls at school. I assumed Diane knew them. I never asked where they came from; I don't know where they went. They were glamorous creatures. Standing tanned shoulder to tanned shoulder on the retired dirt road behind our school, they seemed impervious to the early April chill. They talked in a ring and sighed often, turning colourful plastic bracelets on their slim wrists as they passed around a hand rolled cigarette.

Diane and I fished around our pockets for our money. I smoothed out our crumpled bills between my fingers. Diane gave it all to the tall girl with golden hair. The tall girl had a pointed face, a silver charm bracelet of little crowns and hearts, and a choker necklace. Pocketing the money, she tossed me the pint. I fumbled and almost dropped it. She grinned. Her teeth were straight, but disarmingly yellow and thin, spaces between each one. She smiled like no one had ever noticed.

"Smooth, kid," she said. Her troupe laughed; Diane laughed with them. I didn't know what to say. I stood clutching the pint, wanting to go home. Diane returned a joke with them. I could tell they liked her; I could tell they'd forget me. I wondered when she had learned to be cool like that, and where I had been.

We hid our purchase deep inside Diane's coat and walked too

stiffly all the way home. The drink, when poured, looked like water, and so we mixed it in our glasses, half-and-half, with cool water from the tap. We both marvelled the way it changed: something so clear with something so clear, and then suddenly pearls. It didn't even taste so bad and went down remarkably fast. My hands were the first to feel fuzzy, then my entire face. I felt like I was made of wind.

I don't think I kissed her first. I was never brave enough. But I remember how pink her lips looked as we sat beside each other on the couch, how the moon was almost full, how her eyes kept flicking around my face. But I kissed back, and harder. The couch cushions slipped and parted beneath us while the radio played. When I touched her feathery hair and then slid my other hand up the back of her shirt, she slapped me. She stood up quick.

"Girls just practice kissing," she said. "For later. This isn't real."

"I know that, what do you think we're doing?" I said, scoffing, but I felt achy in my stomach. "It's not real."

Diane's mouth twisted in front of a laugh; I snorted into the back of my hand. We started giggling suddenly, surprised little chirps. I wanted it to feel like we were friends again and put on a movie, but ten minutes later Diane called an older boy. He had a car, a rusting black Stanza with a cheap decal of a sprinting white horse bursting across the front door. He came over, and five minutes after that they were gone. The movie was still playing, but the sound of it only carved out how empty the house was, so I turned it off and went to bed. I had to close my eyes tight to keep the ceiling from spinning.

***

When we buried my grandmother two years ago, the funeral parlour smelled exactly the same. Like powder, wood polish, and dead violets. A well-vacuumed smell. That's the funny thing: it's the things you don't care about that stay the same forever.

***

I don't remember when Diane and I stopped talking to each other. There was no fight; a frictionless gap simply opened between us. I would notice her in the school hallway, but she seemed blind to me. If she or I were in the bathroom at the same time it was to the mirror that we gravitated, applying lipstick or fluffing hair until the other could slip away. I fantasized about fighting, but I knew it was only a dream. Only friends or enemies fight. I was not invited to her sweet-sixteen party, and that evening I was at home watching television.

The next day at school we all found out that she and three others in her boyfriend's car had been killed while driving down the Old Farm Road for extended celebrations.

A giddy buzz ran through the classroom. Everyone was sad that they were dead, but excited that they had been killed. The one girl who survived the crash later said she didn't even remember what happened. When she found herself standing by the wreck, after being thrown from the car, incredibly uninjured, she'd still been laughing at a joke Diane had told. No one liked to hear it, but we were still desperate to be retold, over and over, how Teresa Kelly had still been alive in the backseat as the car burned. Her nail polish had caught on fire along with her hair as she beat on the hot, slick windows. They found Diane's boyfriend's left arm hanging from the tree above the car, like it had tried to climb away without the rest of him. There wasn't much left of anyone else, but there was nothing of Diane, just ash and a warped pair of diamond earrings were found in the charred remains of the front seat.

There was a memorial after school, but I did not go. I bought flowers at the convenience store, the largest bouquet of assorted tulips they had. The sidewalk was hot, the grass around it dry and yellow, and I tied my sweater around my waist as I made my way to Diane's house. I had not been there in three years, and it was not how I remembered it. The lights were all off, and the car was not in the garage. I imagined that if someone were to take off the front wall, cut it neatly away from the roof and peel it back, they would find the whole thing scooped out and empty, like a dollhouse.

I climbed the three chipped cement stairs to the front door. The two tear-drop shaped windows stared blindly back at me. I stood, hand raised to knock, for a long time. The house was more than empty; the silence was a deeper silence. I found I couldn't break that stillness and lowered my hand; too many things break in such simple ways.

I knelt and began to push the flowers through the mail slot instead, gently at first. The petals began to fall; their long green stems bent, their sweet green scent filling the air. The petals bruised. I began to cram the whole bouquet in, pound it with my fist and jab with my chipping fingernails. I skinned my knuckle. I stuck it in my mouth, and it tasted like grass and copper. My fingers became sticky with sap. I picked up every last petal laying on the step, not one left behind, and poked them inside behind the tight metal shutter. When there were no petals left, I ran all the way home.

That night, my mother sat on the edge of my bed, stroking my hair.

"It is so hard to lose such a good friend," she told me. Her hand stayed, just for an instant. "Your good friend."

I didn't say anything.

I nodded.

***

I was seventeen when one of the boys came back.

Mom was still at work, and I was home alone and washing the dishes. It was November, and the sky was a cold, fish-belly grey, the trees bare and stiff. The jack-o-lantern I had carved for Halloween had been taken to the edge of our property, to the kissing gate. That mouldering orange face, staring wanly at the sky, was the only bit of colour I could see through the warm steam rising around my chin and eyes. My hands were immersed deep into the sudsy dishwater. I was almost finished and feeling around for the dishcloth when I looked up and saw green and blue where there had not been any green and blue before. I stared at him. He noticed me and stared back. After a moment, he started walking up the path towards our house.

I pulled my hands from the water, flicked them off, and then dried them on my jeans. I went to the sliding door at the other side of the kitchen and unlocked it. I made a pair of tuna sandwiches, cutting them diagonally, and poured two short glasses of orange juice.

When I turned back around and set the plates down on the small kitchen island, he was stepping inside and carefully wiping his muddy sneakers on the doormat. He looked up at me. He was skinny, and just the same (and not at all the same) as I remembered. Pulling on the bottom of his rocket sweater, he looked around the kitchen, and then to the plates. Without a word, he walked to the island, sat down on a stool, and began to eat his sandwich. I stood on the other side of the island to eat mine.

"I remember you," I said. The boy just nodded, as though in agreement.

When he finished and was drinking his juice, I asked him how old he was. He set down his glass and looked up. His large brown eyes were cradled in soft, purple sleeplessness. He pressed his lips flat, thinking. After a minute, he said he wasn't sure anymore. He drank the last of his juice. Eleven, he decided finally. I nodded and agreed that that sounded right. I asked where his friend was.

"He stayed," he replied. "Usually they stay with her." He glanced all around the kitchen—from the new dishwasher, to the old, heavy laptop on the counter—with an air of disappointment and sighed. "I should go home now."

He got up with his plate and mine, put them in the sink for me, and then he went back to the sliding door.

"Wait," I said. The boy stopped, looked back a moment, and then left.

There were two dishes in the sink. There were two glasses on the counter, sticky orange juice drying in the bottoms. On the rung of one of the stools there were two muddy tracks. I cleaned everything and put the dishes away. When I was done, it was like it had never happened. I watched the local news carefully that evening with my mother. She commented that I was getting so grown up. When I didn't see anything reported about the boy, I decided that I wouldn't say anything at all. I really don't know why now, but I knew then. I knew exactly why.

***

Sometimes when I dream the person I am isn't me; sometimes I don't know who it is. It was like that. I crossed the yard the night after the boy came back, in my pyjamas and feet bare, and curled my hands around the top of the iron gate to peer down the path in the pine woods. There was no moon, but the sky glowed a faded lavender, and I could see. It was deeply cold. It started to snow a little, slow, tiny flakes. The snow fell around the yard behind me, through the trees, and down the path in front of me, spinning above the frozen ground. I had not expected to see anyone, but I was not surprised when I did.

They filled the lane, hundreds of them, all the way back, all staring with sleepless eyes. The snow danced around their feet in dusty swirls. The closest two held hands. One looked beautiful, the way I always remember her—except her eyes; they were exactly like the faded November sky behind her. The other had tumbling golden hair, a crown of silver and bone, perfect and hideous teeth, and a smile that was too excited to be kind. She was the only one looking at me. She reached out her hand. I tried to let go of the gate. My skin pulled and stuck, like it was glued there. I brought my mouth close to my fingers and breathed on them to warm the iron. Something sharp caressed my ear, and I let go, stepping back quickly. The pathway was empty, and quietly filling with snow.

I went back inside.

When I woke the next morning I was in my bed, and the world had become muffled with snow. I sat looking out my window for a long time, but there was no evidence of where or if I'd been to the gate; clean white covered all like a new page.

***

I have a picture on my wall of two little girls grinning like lunatics, swinging their legs over the ledge of an unfinished patio while vanilla ice-creams drool down their wrists. One of the girls is me, although we look nothing alike. I don't remember being her at all. I would not let ice-cream melt down my arm like that, and I would not grin with both rows of teeth like that—tiny teeth that I don't even have anymore. But it must be true, because there we are. A little girl with whom I share a past, but perhaps nothing else.

FORGETTING LEVIATHAN

1

On a bright day, many years ago, a monster washed up on the shores of Saint-Andrews-by-the-Sea. The creature (barnacle mottled and fog white) bumped on the jagged beach stones with every lazy slosh of the waves. The behemoth's loose jaw hung open, gargling the tide and a feast of rockweed and pebbles, the skin at the corners of its mouth was torn and ragged. Its dozen small, black eyes had succumbed to a thick layer of opaque mucus and mirrored many twisted, white reflections of the morning sun. Sinewy, clawed hands twisted awkwardly underneath its bloated belly. The webbing between its fingers was as broken as old lace, and its once-powerful tail mashed into fleshy pulp. Crabs clicked methodically around it, gulls lighted on its back in ecstatic panic, all stripped off rubbery chunks by beak and claw.

It was this cacophony that drew the boys.

2

The two boys, sons of farm labourers from the adjacent Minister's Island, had been walking along the train tracks. The hard soles of Andy's boots slipped slightly as he walked, arms aloft, on the hot, shiny rails. Frankie made long strides between the ties, his hands crammed deep in the pockets of his woolen short-pants. The hot air of the tracks rose and wavered before them like the memory of water. They were not supposed to be there. The tracks curved along the edge of the bay and as neither could swim well they had been strictly instructed by both of their mothers to avoid the water's edge, lest a rogue wave reach out and carry them away. But it was a beautiful day, and the boys knew with the solid certainty of childhood that nothing bad could happen to them.

3

Saint-Andrews-by-the-Sea is a Loyalist settlement established on a little spear of land darting out into the cold Atlantic Ocean, pointing towards the American coast like an accusing finger.

Everyone who grows up there swears they'll leave as soon as they can; almost everyone who leaves comes back, sure as driftwood on the tide. A good place to raise a family, the townspeople agree when they all inevitably see each other again.

A good place.

In the 1850s, ship after ship of Irish immigrants started showing up at the town's little harbour and wharf. Those who hadn't, for reasons of illness or madness, had been shown the shores of a small quarantine island several sullen sail flaps north of where Andy and Frankie would decades later walk and a monster would die.

There were only guesses at how many people had been quarantined on the island. The number was always more than folks of the time were quite comfortable with. The island sat staring at the mainland and the mainland turned its shoulder. The town grew as the forgotten little island's population did what it was intended to do.

4

The two boys who were soon to find the monster started their walk at the very tip of the peninsular town. Their original objective had been the northern shore of the swimming cove, where their hopes of spotting some of the summer ladies lay waiting. Tommy LeBlanc had sworn, cross-his-heart, that they now did their sunning in *two-piece* bathing suits. He had then added, a little too eagerly to be believed, that sometimes they even strutted around the beach naked. Frankie had shoved him then and said that he was full of it before swaggering off to find Andy. A lead like that was still too good to ignore—even if it did come from a rag-arsed little weirdo like Tommy. Rich folks got up to all kinds of strange things when they thought no one was looking.

The cove was a disappointment. Not only were the ladies fully clothed (as far as they could tell, at least) but they were barely visible across the kilometre of salty water that separated the railbed from the private portion of the beach. At that distance, they could hardly see a thing, they didn't even seem real.

Disenchanted, the boys continued down the tracks and decided that they would wait on Sir William Van Horne's personal train platform while the tide went down, and then try to sneak across the Bar Road onto the island. The railway executive (their fathers' employer and owner of the island) would soon be arriving for the summer with his family, and the boys figured they would likely not have another chance to trespass until the winter.

They made their way to the small, unattended platform and it was from there that they heard the frenzied flocking of seagulls, and further on found the body of the monster.

5

The boys approached slowly, reverently. A congregation of gulls lifted, squalling, from their altar; their devotion drew them back, no more disturbed by the boys than they were of the sand beetles that crawled in and out of the creature's mangled tail. The boys stared up at the ashen body, the flabby gills, and the crowded mouth of needle-like teeth. Wordlessly, they linked hands.

"Is it dead?" said Andy. He then wondered aloud if they should find a stick to prod it with, just to check, but neither one acted on this proposal. Frankie let go of Andy's hand, took a step closer, and then hunkered down, hands easy between his knees, to look at it more closely. He'd seen his father do this when inspecting things: busted tractor wheel, a fallen calf.

"Let's go home," said Andy. "We'll get in trouble."

"Can't get in trouble just for finding something," Frankie replied sagely.

"Yes, you can. Let's just forget it." He paused. Frankie jumped back as Andy suddenly screamed, nearly slipping on the rockweed.

"Faces! In the skin, look at the faces!"

Frankie spun around. He couldn't see any faces.

"It's just rot," he said. "Skin's all flyblown, see." He leaned closer.

"People faces, it eats people!"

"If it did, it's dead now." Frankie looked back and saw his friend running as fast as he could, not down the tracks but up the dirt road towards town. He knew this meant Andy was running for an adult and he felt deeply betrayed. Frankie started to jog after his friend but abruptly stopped.

There were sounds coming from the creature.

At first, he thought it was the grinding rocks beneath it, or the chatter of the seagulls atop it. Frankie drew closer, listening; the reek was powerful. The noise grew no louder, but somehow denser, like a huge, grinding millstone. He could hear it in his chest, in his skull. He laid one hand on the creature's cold, rough skin and his shadow disappeared beneath his ear as he placed his cheek upon its body. Bones creaked inside, like ship masts in a storm; gases churned like crashing waves, sickly moans; squealing like wind, like screams lost on a profound, black ocean.

6

A buggy came rattling down the narrow dirt road, its windshield winking in the bright sunlight. It chugged to a stop and the two men inside climbed out. They found the boy a little up the shoreline, sitting atop a large boulder. His eyes were dark and intent as he stared at the bay, the wet clicks of the crabs and gasping caws of the gulls all around, his knees pulled up to his chin. They began to ask if he was friends with the boy who had come screaming into town but abruptly ended their questioning with the well-oiled vocabulary of seafaring men.

One man picked Frankie up and put him on the back of the buggy while the other gawked. The boy said he needed to watch the water, but the man in the buggy told him he was going back to his mother.

"It is a mother," the boy said. The man slapped him. Later, the man, Tim Martin, would swear the chid had felt somehow hollow, like slapping the side of a dead log.

As the buggy zipped away, spinning gravel and seaweed beneath its narrow tires, the boy looked back through the wind-whipped lanks of his sandy hair, watching the creature disappear behind a rise of red sandstone.

"You don't be telling anyone about this," said the other man, Burt Renshaw. "Not a soul until we figure this out."

The boy looked up at the men with his dark, distant eyes.

They needn't have worried that the boy would talk, as it turned out. Frankie spent the rest of the week seeing and speaking to no one, not even Andy when he came around, and then he was sent to work with his father, mucking out stalls on Minister's Island. First day at work, he was brained by a horse that had never spooked in its life. A sour breeze had risen from the bay as the boy stood staring at the sea from the stable doors—before turning and heading straight for the horse. A farmhand who'd seen it all confessed later to his wife that the boy, who had worked with the animals in the past, had gone for the horse, shovel in hand, a sound like a gale wind whistling through a broken window rasping from the boy's small, pale mouth.

"I'd never say it," he whispered in bed, "but what a relief when that horse kicked his face in, stopped that unnatural noise."

Andy, devastated by the loss and confused by the grief, never spoke of his friend again and did his best to forget him, and all they'd done and seen, forever.

7

Martin and Renshaw, the men from the buggy, having no wish to start dark rumours about something as important to the town as the sea, were discreet. They delivered the strange boy to his mother and within the half-hour they had made two stops. The first was to the home of Mayor Hyde. The mayor had just sat down to a late breakfast and was in the process of cracking an egg when the two men entered his drawing room clutching their hats and begging his pardon. After they had explained the urgency of the matter the three men sought out the only man they supposed might be of any further use: Mr. Callow, the Wharfinger.

Mr. Callow was a gaunt man with long white whiskers and a mouth like the slash of a knife. He had been a sailor for years and had forgotten more than most would ever know about the ocean. He had sailed when the tall ships ruled the seas, but now was retired to the docks. If anyone would know the beast, it was him.

The men approached the wharfinger's hut at the end of the wharf with not just a little fear and awe and described the matter.

"No beast like that," the Wharfinger told them. "T'is a whale."

They begged him to see for himself, before the tide turned. After he'd seen to the custody of one more dory, he allowed himself to be led from his post at the end of the Market Wharf down to the Bar Road. When he saw the enormous flotsam, he was at as much of a loss as they were. Mr. Callow and Mayor Hyde exited the automobile and made to take a closer look; Martin and Renshaw, freshly nauseated with the smell and sight, stayed in the buggy.

The tide was still due to rise, and the mayor was able to walk the full circle of the creature, only dampening the edges of his boots in the shallow tidal pools. He returned to Callow's side, pulling on his bristly black moustache while the thin habourmaster stared, as stuck-still as an old weir post. Clouds stretched in front of the sun, darkening the beach. The wind began to low in the warm air. The smell drifted and Mayor Hyde stepped back, knocked from his contemplation by the stench.

"You will be sure to tell everyone that proper care was taken in the disposing of the whale," he said.

Callow sniffed. "Not a whale." He retrieved a small pipe and matchbook from his breast pocket and set it to the groove in his teeth.

"You said it yourself earlier."

"Aye, I did." He lit the pipe. "Not a whale."

Mayor Hyde gave him a cool look. "And have you ever seen a whale above the waves, Mr. Callow?"

"Don't be afraid, mister mayor," said Callow, shaking his match dead, "but there's more than whales to see below the waves."

Mayor Hyde made a noise of irritation and surveyed the beast with a stout ducking of his lips. His considerable moustache bristled out like the feelers of a lobster. A spot of rain darkened the shoulder of his coat. Another pecked the brim of Callow's black cap.

"The Royal Society is, even as we speak, devising ways to drop great lengths of telegraph cable along the ocean floor and designing new submersibles to do so. I shouldn't be surprised if a dozen more of these creatures were uncovered by the end of the decade. They will prove to be more common than crabs."

"Then I shouldn't like to be in the water much," Callow said.

Mayor Hyde directed a hand to the deceased. "Anyone can see from the size that it is a creature of the deep and poses no real threat to anyone on shore. Its presence here is a grim marvel, but of no real concern to anyone and best forgotten."

"If you say."

"I say get rid of it." The mayor turned, fetching a handkerchief and pressing it to his lips and forehead as he trudged up the rocky beach to the Bar Road. "By tomorrow," he puffed. "I'm putting you in charge. Hire reasonable men to assist you."

"Its tail," Callow commented. "Looks half bitten away. What did that, do you imagine?"

"I don't imagine," said the mayor, not turning. "Not while reality remains substantive. Good luck with the whale."

The four men left the secluded beach again with the intention of immediately gathering more men with wagons and trucks to help to parcel up and remove the remains. But by the time they reached the town the wind had picked up, the rain had begun to whip, and no one could be convinced to risk the steep route down to the Bar to painstakingly chop up some dead whale.

8

The storm rattled the town throughout the day, and well into the night, flooding the main street to such a degree that fish were found gasping in the road for days following. Mrs. Grace Powell's dog was swept away, and the windows of Town Hall were cracked in a surge and had become littered with seaweed and salt. No one could remember such a vicious storm.

The next morning, depleted clouds hung overhead like wrung dishcloths. The air had chilled, and many people wondered out loud how they ever could have thought that it would be a hot summer. The townsfolk threw on sweaters and forgetting the heat of only the day before, grumbled about what a cold season it was shaping up to be.

9

Callow found nearly half a dozen men to help him dispose of the creature. Only Renshaw and Martin were locals, the other three were drifters from Maine and New Hampshire, come north in search of summer work.

The rain and the high tide had altered the beach. Pebbles shifted and squelched beneath the men's work boots as they walked down the shore. When they came to the small recess on the eastern side of the Bar Road, the carcass was no longer there. They spotted the thing another twenty metres down, closer to the low-tide line. The night tide had dragged it over the stones and spun it around so that its ruined tail faced them. It almost appeared as if the thing had tried to crawl back into the sea.

But as the men approached with shovels and axes hefted on their shoulders, they saw that it was just as dead as they had been promised.

Callow came to the front of the team and gazed at the advanced putrefaction of the single night. One of its knotted arms had broken off and lay beside its torn belly. One side of the creature had collapsed, its broken ribs pushing the white skin from beneath like shattered masts stabbing against a giant sail.

The number of snails, crabs, fleas, and beetles swarming the beast was enormous. The hiss and click of their collective efforts were louder than the steady shush of the tide itself. Parasites made a mess of its face; the seagulls had not left their vigil and stood lined upon the back of their prize. The thinning flesh writhed from beneath, puckering with unseen things.

"It's moving," said one of the men, voice hushed.

"Just crabs," said Martin, holding his shovel in both hands like a woodman's axe. He nervously licked his upper lip. "They got inside, is all."

Callow peered at the crabs. The small creatures were trimming away the flesh, careful as seamstresses. Once they had cut a manageable portion, they lifted it over their shells rather than pack their morsel into their small pincer mouths, and then scuttled quickly away without eating. He watched their progress and observed them forming long trickling lines, rushing back to the water with bits of flesh and bone, like ants marching through a field. Three gulls took flight, flew far out over the bay and, without fighting, dropped their fragments softly onto the water.

"Why don't they eat it?" said Martin.

"Not too bright, these birds," commented one of the American labourers in a bold tone that fooled no one. He walked up to the side of the body and raised a hand to pat the carcass experimentally—and jumped out of the way as one of the birds dove at him.

A few men chuckled, but without much humor. Another man approached the creature's mouth, bopping the butt of his hatchet in one hand. "Would you boys mind me taking some of these here teeth?" He hefted the axe, swinging it down at the exposed jaw.

Feathers burst in a red spray.

A seagull dove in front of the blade, and was split nearly in two. The man swore and staggered backwards, his face and lips freckled with blood. The gull dropped to the rocks, the two halves twitching and flapping. More gulls launched themselves at the man, shrieking, pecking, and beating their wings. He dropped his axe and raised his arms to shield his face, running back to the others, who themselves retreated further in a cluster. When the man reached them, Martin simply dropped his shovel and walked at a quick pace back towards town.

"Not supposed to be things like that," they heard him remark. "And I don't want to see or know it."

No one stopped him. Someone asked if they could split his pay.

The others turned their attention back to the creature and saw the birds had redoubled their efforts, pulling off larger chunks of flesh, cartilage, and meat from the decaying form with fresh urgency.

"Crazed birds," observed one man.

"We've got to get rid of that thing," said Renshaw.

"Leave it," said the man who'd split the bird. He held his bleeding face where a gull's foot had raked him. He spat. "Damn the whale."

But the bleeding man did not leave and join Martin.

The man waited for the old wharfinger to give an order. He had not run as they had, and still stood quite close to the creature.

"Mr. Callow?" said Renshaw, finally.

The wharfinger did not take his eyes away from the giant. The men exchanged looks. The sky darkened, the waves took on a heavy green hue, and through the noise of the gulls and waves there came a steady howling, like a strong wind over rocks—although the pines lining the shore were steady and sober.

"All things return to the sea, gentlemen," said Callow in voice soft as waterlogged timbers, empty as wind through a moored hull.

The remaining men shuffled their feet. At last, Renshaw, face pale, hands shaking, took up a fallen shovel. The other three followed as his feet lead him unwillingly towards the creature, towards the low steady howling.

10

It was late at night before anyone in town saw Callow. The old wharfinger walked the length of Water Street, his hands hanging, his eyes the glassy pink of a gutted fish. The pub, the Heron's Nest, was not yet closed and he let himself in and helped himself to a sticky bar stool. He asked for a bottle of lager and stared at it.

Martin approached him from the other side of the bar and leaned on the counter next to him. "How'd the job go?"

The old man only stared, a sound coming from his lips, cold and whistling.

"Where's Burt?"

The murmurs and sticky cracks of the old man's throat went on uninterrupted. Martin slammed down his own bottle, frothing the suds, and left the pub.

In time, the old man was noticed by others, muttering into the green neck of his untouched lager. When he had completed his clandestine sermon, he began again, and then again. His eyes remained wide and unseeing. A pair of men who had been requested but declined the expedition, leaned over, deep in their cups, and asked with broad smiles whether he had taken care of the whale.

"The water never forgets," Callow said, uninterrupted. "But takes and shapes anew."

"Sure, whales beach all the time," said the older of the two, laughing.

"They went to the creature and took to it with axes and shovels, depositing it as they could to the waves. Renshaw was the first to see. Not one thing anymore, but many in one."

The older drunk's eyebrows dipped momentarily with concern, but the barmaid nudged him cheekily as she walked by, and he spun around, distracted.

"They took it apart. Piece by piece," Callow told his bottle. "The bones they carried with their hands, and the sounds they carried within them. A thousand deaths on the sea, and what the sea swallows, it keeps. What it touches, it takes. It took their minds as sure it took their bodies. The last to go was the heart. It was dark and hard and black, not at all like the thing itself. It came away in many pieces. Layers and layers and layers ..."

"So, there will be nothing unpleasant for Sir William to see tomorrow?" asked the other drunk man.

"After they had taken all the creature and all within it back to the water, they began on one another. Renshaw was the first to fall, taking his hand then arm, a strip of flesh from the leg and the sinews of his chest. The young one broke his own nose inwards with the back of his axe until t'were not but a bloody blowhole. One by one, they took themselves apart. The last man parceled them off and the crabs did the rest. Then he lay himself down in the water and the current took him under. The bay pulsed once like a heart that skipped a beat and she rose once to the surface, more than she was. I wanted to go with her, but she left me to watch, to see, to bring her to land. She'll come again. She'll rise again. All things return to the sea, and when she rises again, we'll all return with her."

The two men had been joking with the barmaid for some time. Callow began to repeat his tale, but songs had begun, and no one cared to hear what an old man had to say twice.

11

The next morning the Van Horne family arrived at their private station and took their fine carriages across the Bar Road to their summer home. The town paper reported of the beaching and successful disposal of a whale near the same.

12

The body of Mr. Callow was discovered near the wharf a week later. The body, pale and bloated nearly beyond recognition, was discovered by two young girls as they searched for seashells.

IT'S A HELLUVA THING, BILL

It had never been anything more than a dirt floor basement and Bill Morgan had always taken an elemental pride in that. He didn't go down there very often so he wasn't sure just when the gateway had opened, but he figured it must have been in the early fall, after school had started; his sister regularly brought her kids over to play during the summer and they would have said something. They were always hurrying down into the cool, subterranean darkness, Evelyn shouting after them not to just as fast as they went anyway.

"Kids are animals," Bill would say with a chuckle, cracking a beer as she cracked him a scowl. "They need the dirt every now and then."

"Too early for that," she would murmur, or "It's the Lord's Day." But Bill would lean back in his kitchen chair, grinning, his moustache frothing with suds, content in the knowledge that the sun was hot, the bugs were low, and the Sea Dogs were having a good season.

When it got chillier, September being a fickle but fine season in New Brunswick, Evelyn still brought the kids over to see Uncle Bill, but then they mostly stayed out of the basement and in the TV room pretending to do their homework, playing Minesweeper on his ancient computer, or wringing out the last of the long days with a protracted game of tag out in the backyard. Bill would make coffee and Evelyn would accept a cup, fixing it with a neat dob of milk.

Bill had steady blue eyes and looked like the kind of man who took his coffee black, but in fact loaded it with so much cream and sugar you could stand a knife up in it. At least three days of stubble always stood out all over his large, round face, and a bristly moustache curled like a sleeping dog under his lumpy red nose. His high, wide forehead was forever squeezed into an old hunting cap which had started off in this world red flannel but was now so covered in engine oil and sawdust that it was a hard call at a glance. His hands were huge and he held everything like it were a small, trembling bird.

"You and the kids gonna be over on Thanksgiving?" Bill had asked during their last visit, slurping his coffee. The screen door had snapped open as the three kids chased each other inside, laughing breathlessly.

"You kids stay out of there," their mother had intoned automatically as they disappeared, unheeding, down the basement stairs. Evelyn sat up a little straighter, adjusted the slim, gold bracelet on her narrow wrist, and told him that the kids would be with their father that weekend. She did not say where she would be. Bill said nothing and drank his coffee. They were quiet a while.

After a minute, they glanced around at the silence. The kids were no longer playing. Kitchen chairs squeaking, Bill and Evelyn turned to look towards the basement.

The three kids stood in a line at the top of the stairs. Hanging from the hand of the youngest was what, for a second, looked like an empty, hairy potato sack. But just for a second.

Evelyn screamed. She jumped up and slapped it from her little boy's hand, wildly warning, "Rabies!"

Bill went down basement to investigate further, down the cracked linoleum steps as Evelyn gathered up coats and demanded shoes on everyone before they got back into the car.

Through the small basement window, he heard the middle child appeal to her mother's reason. "But it's dead, mom," said Madeline. "Ain't gonna hurt no one."

Bill had always liked her.

"Doesn't matter, and don't talk like that. You sound like a hick."

"Uncle Bill talks like that and he's smart. He's got all those cool books in his TV room —"

A thin snap sounded. The girl began revving up to a real red-faced bawl.

"You—You shouldn't be touching a grown-up's things," Evelyn said, by way of explanation.

Bill listened to the car pull out of the driveway as he descended the rest of stairs. He flicked on the light; a naked bulb sparked and popped dead. He stuck two fingers under the rim of his cap and scratched his head as he squinted through the dark. But even by the dusty light of the small basement windows, he could see there was no hole for the thing to have gotten in by. And nothing for it to have hidden under or become stuck behind. The only things in the room were some old cinder blocks, a rolled length of chicken wire, and the furnace.

Bill worked his way back up the stairs, panting a little by the time he reached the landing, and then dug a garbage bag out from under the kitchen sink. Reaching his arms inside the bag, he scooped up the dry body from where it still lay on his kitchen floor and pulled it inside. Static caught its mangy fur as he inverted the bag and it stiffly slid to the bottom.

The weasel was as big as a terrier and black as a leech. Ugly sonovagun in death, but even alive it would've been no cutie. Small yellow teeth snarled out from a warped mouth; its ears were pus-filled sores; its eyes were crusty bug-holes. One gnarly paw had dried crooked against its twisted shoulder, like old roadkill. Poor wretch must have been down there for a while and, by the look of things, starved to death. But why it hadn't just to come up the stairs was beyond Bill. He usually left a roast chicken out on the counter after Sundays as a little something to pick at during the week. Why hadn't it come sniffing around?

He tied the bag off and walked the thing to his dented aluminum garbage can at the edge of the driveway, dropping it on a chiming chorus of cans and bottles.

He considered the bag momentarily and wondered if someone would like to look at the thing, maybe he'd call up the University ... But these days he was a practical man. He banged the lid on the can and by week's end, he'd forgotten the whole thing.

***

It was the smell that alerted him that something wasn't right. Low, acidic, and eggy. It was a cold morning, the first frost had fallen overnight, and no scent had any business being so powerful when he could practically see his breath as he hauled himself out of bed. He followed the sulphur stink, nose raised and nostrils flared, to his basement.

The first thing he noticed was the warmth. Normally at this time of year, the cellar was as cold as a witch's tit, but today it was as pleasant as a pussycat. A whistling moan, like wind through a slit window, hummed in flat loops behind the furnace. Bill approached with a hand over his nose and mouth, and there discovered a plywood board (so covered in dirt he could barely see it) on the floor. The noise, and the smell, was coming from underneath. Bill flipped the board aside. Hot air enveloped him.

Turned out, it wasn't just the wind.

The fiery chasm spiralled down to the very bowels of the earth, a narrow channel lined with flames and thorns of black flint. Down and down and down the chasm, naked, moaning bodies lay splayed across the barbed rocks, or impaled and dangling. The crackling, red under-light illuminated Bill's ponderous jowls and the little fuzzies on the beak of his cap. His eyes grew wide. He hunkered down, pressed the palms of his hands together like a man about to start a prayer ... and then drew them apart. He would have to bring a tape measurer down later, but he could do with a rough estimate for now.

Had Bill not leaned back on the furnace a second later, using it to push himself to his feet, the creature would have clawed right into him. The thing shot out of the fissure like the allegorical bat out of hell that it was, hitting the roof of the basement with a back-breaking snap and fell fast to the floor. The bat, the size of an open umbrella, flopped spasmodically. Suddenly, it shrivelled to nothing, ribs standing out in a starved stack, its knotted spinal column popping up under its bristly fur like a huge worm ready to break free of wet earth. Its black eyes protruded, and, with an almost human expression of surprise, died.

It all happened too fast for Bill to have taken any proper alarm, and now that it was over he wasn't about to get busy being upset. He chewed the side of his cheek and consider the beast. He remembered he was all out of garbage bags.

"Aw, hell," he said, finally swaying to his feet. But what was left of the bat was already dryer than a popcorn fart, and he decided it wouldn't hurt anything to leave it where it was for now.

The heat shimmering out of the hole had been so fine that when he got back to the chilly upstairs, he was rubbing one elbow and thinking wistfully about his old polar fleece fishing jacket. He dug it out of the closet and put it on before he made his phone call.

Larry Fisher picked up on the third ring.

"Got a little something I figure I'll need a hand with," Bill said. "Bring your tools."

Larry's rusted blue work van rattled down the gravel drive-way an hour later.

Bill was sitting at the kitchen table sipping thoughtfully at a can of Moosehead when the door opened. Larry came in, stamping his feet like they were covered in snow.

"Nippy one today, eh?" said Larry. "Got something for me to look at?"

Bill offered him a beer. "We'll get to it."

The two men sat and drank in silence. Although not yet quite sixty, Larry's skin hung loose on his bones and blue under his hangdog eyes. His snowy hair was thinning, revealing a spotted scalp. Bill thought that there were even more lines pinched around the repairman's face since last time they dealt out for a round of gin rummy.

"You sick, Lare?"

"Nah," he said, plinking at the tab on his empty can. "Long days, is all. Alice's found the religion. Ever since the cancer. She likes that old stuff."

Bill nodded and drew a long slurp. "Aww," he said, almost weary, "it's all tenacious as a tick."

"I didn't really approve at first," Larry went on, "but the doctor said it would help Alice's recovery for me to take an interest in her hobbies too. Support, right? I didn't really get it at first, but I've been doing the readings lately. And I like it, I actually like it." He grinned. "And those churchy ladies sure can bake a macaroon."

Larry's chair trumpeted on the linoleum as he pushed it back. "Well, I'll get my tools," he said. "Let's take a look at this furnace of yours."

The two men stood at the lip of the fissure. Larry's eyes bugged out in almost exactly the same way as the giant bat's had done, his mouth stretching down into a long, dark zero of amazement. "Merciful God," he whispered. "It's all true."

Bill sniffed, crossed his arms as best he could athwart his ample chest, and waited for Larry to get it out of his system.

"What I figure," Bill said, tapping the cold metal side of the rusty furnace behind them (it *blong-blong*ed like a drum), "is that this could really help cut down on my heating bill this winter."

Larry's head slowly turned his way. It looked like something done at great personal cost. He stared at Bill with confounded eyes.

Bill held out his hand. "Feel the heat coming off of this thing?"

A high shriek echoed out of the depths.

Larry's eyebrows dipped into puzzled rivets. He stared at Bill a moment longer, and then also extended his hand. He eventually nodded.

"Radiating, even, and—from the looks of it—sustainable. I was thinking." He affectionately patted the wood furnace again.

"Might just be able to route a duct to this here. Maybe add a damper so I can set how much heat is coming out." He crossed his arms again and added softly to his thoughts. "Throw a grate over it, maybe install some sort of filter for the smell. That's the ticket, I reckon. What do you think?"

Larry continued to stare at Bill, amazed. "You want a heating duct?"

"Sure do."

"Connect this to your wood furnace?"

Bill chuckled. "You're the expert on these things."

"What's the matter with you?" said Larry, almost angry.

Bill shrugged, and said not without sympathy, "It is what it is, Lare."

Larry looked at the dead bat beside them on the floor. He had stepped over it to get to the hole but hadn't really looked at it. "Uninvited guest?"

"Yeah," said Bill, tugging at the seat of this pants. His crotch was sweating from standing so close to the burning chasm. "And a weasel like you wouldn't believe before it. This one died in just about five seconds. Weasel probably went the same way."

"And what about them?"

"Who?"

Larry directed a hand to the naked, moaning bodies thirty feet down.

Bill shook his head ruefully. Nothing to be done.

Now Larry crossed his arms and considered the matter.

"Things come up and die. You tried dropping something down?" He eyed a couple good rocks scattered around the floor. Bill chuckled and slapped Larry on the shoulder, who lurched forward. He shot Bill a sour look.

"Know the four best words in the English language?" Bill replied. "Don't. Mess. With. It."

Larry sighed and tipped his old blue Yankees cap back. "It's a helluva thing, Bill."

Bill laughed again. "Yeah."

"You told anyone else about this?"

"No." He thought about mentioning how someone would want to send a bunch of scientists in, or police, or priests, or a combination of the three—he'd personally known the type—and they'd all start digging around, as excited as a bunch of gerbils in new pine shavings. But said instead, "They'd just find a way to tax me for it."

Larry considered the fiery pit once more. "Yeah, I reckon you're onto something." He licked his bottom lip. "I reckon something ought to be done."

Larry left. Bill waved goodbye at the door, but the scrawny repairman walked flat-footed to his truck. The driver's side door squealed as he opened it. He paused with one leg in the cab and looked around.

"You have a good night, Bill." His mouth worked a moment. "I hear there's a good movie playing down in Fredericton tonight. Got that funny lady in it."

Bill stuck the tips of his fingers in his pockets. "Naw," said Bill. "Top of the Hanwell is looking like the ass-end of the moon and the truck's suspension is shot as it is."

"There's the river road, then. Easier driving. Maybe you should go see that movie. Take your mind off this for a bit."

Bill stared after him.

"Maybe I will, Lare."

The old repairman got in his seat and drove off. Bill watched the way he went for a full minute after the sound of the car had dissipated before at last turning back inside his house.

Bill dug a frozen pork chop from his deepfreeze, nuked it in his old microwave, and threw it to sizzle in a skillet. He boiled a potato and ate his meal on the sagging couch in front of the TV.

Just before eleven, he heard his garbage cans tip over.

The springs in the couch chattered when he eventually laid down and clicked off the lamp. His chapped, pink hands cuddled together on his chest like two dozing animals as he began to snore.

***

Bill slept like the dead. Storms could approach, scream for his attention, finally fade and die for spite and he wouldn't so much as twitch. Once he'd had a dog, a mangy, snaggle-tooth mutt he called Hank. Hank had, through some hitherto unknown blaze of intelligence, one night worked the back door open; a skunk had been rooting around the backyard for nightcrawlers, and Hank meant to have it. The dog had torn after the terrified polecat and chased the damned thing right back into the house, barking and raising Cain while his terrified quarry had screeched a high, pleading appeal for mercy from dog, or god, or both, all the while pissing his vast reserves of sweetly-sick skunk musk. Bill had heard none of it. What he woke to in the morning was a stink strong enough to burn the hairs from the nostrils, a disembowelled living room, and a dead dog. The exhausted skunk had sat in the middle of the floor, looking up at Bill with an expression that assured him that it was just as amazed as he was.

Bill could sleep through anything.

Later, Bill figured it must have meant that he was never really asleep that night, because at the first chime he was awake.

Bill sat up. It was dark outside, but the moon was full and it cast a hollow, clear light through his windows. A low, rolling noise came from the basement and he decided to investigate.

They were really going at it by the time he had lumbered down the stairs and spotted them. A small cluster of people were gathered, kneeling, around the crack in his floor. One of the women turned and half-rose as the bottom step creaked under Bill's slippered foot. He recognized her to be Wendy McIntyre, the lady who ran the book mobile. Her normally poofed hair was long and lank; instead of her usual stockings, skirt and starched blouse, she was naked. Her breasts hung like two half-filled water balloons over a wrinkled stomach and an old caesarean scar. She grinned, and a low giggle burbled from her chest, alerting the others. Larry looked up, startled, from the mess of chicken bones and entrails he had been sorting through; two of the other three worshippers also looked around. Alice Fisher, in the proper throws of religious ecstasy, was not to be distracted. The other two, one younger, one older than Bill, but both strangers, turned tentatively back to the pit, unsure of what to make of the intruder. They resumed their chants in their strange, flabby language. There wasn't a thread of clothing between the five people.

"You folks know what you're doing?" Bill asked Larry. Larry stared up again from the chicken bones, bright red sinew still clinging to them, brown feathers sticking to his knees.

"The Boundless Ones arise, Bill," he said, eyes wide and wondering. "Right here, tonight!"

Bill sat down on the bottom step. He reached under his cap and pulled out a crumpled old pack of Nifty Fifties, the high-tar variety, and the lighter he always kept stored with the cigs. He stuck one in his mouth and lit up. "Okay," he said and began doodling on the dirt in front of him with one finger.

"The interloper mocks our faith," declared the young stranger.

"Shut up, Mark," advised the old stranger. "And you sound like a jackass, using words like that. We're in *his* damn furnace room."

The young man set a sulking look on the older man, and then turned back to his chanting.

The dirt of the floor had churned up some sharp rocks with their crawling; they sweated and moaned. They bowed and writhed. When Bill was nearing the filter of his second cigarette, the older man complained loudly that his knees hurt.

"There is something wrong," Alice said, sitting upright, her face contorted with effort and monstrous fervor. Her remaining breast bobbed, her short white and blonde hair glowed in a fiery halo around her wrinkled face. Her eyes were round as she lifted her hands.

"Are we not the faithful?"

"Yes," they chorused back.

"Are we not truly the chosen?"

"Yes!"

"Have we not seen through the blinding wickedness of Light! Understood how only in the Dark may you be truly free!"

"Yes!"

"Free to sing the names of the True Ones, the Boundless! Say so!"

"So, oh, it is So!"

"Sacrifice!" she screamed, taking up the knife that had used to dispatch the hen. The young man threw himself without hesitation in front of her, exposing his sunken ribs and belly, his penis a rigid exclamation mark. Alice drove the carving knife into the young man's pale abdomen and ripped upwards in one savage yank. Bill considered the tips of his calloused fingers as the young man gurgled sharply, a noise that was an uncomfortable species of pleasure and sob.

When the wet gurgles had at last subsided, Bill looked up. The remaining practitioners were crimson up to their elbows. The older man was holding a chunk of something red and slippery, staring at it like he had no idea how it had gotten there.

"What's wrong?" Wendy breathed. She looked down at her hands. "What's wrong!"

"I knew we should have consulted the Elders first," complained the old man, throwing down the hunk of Mark. It hit the torn cavity with a dull little *smack*. The dead young man's blood snaked in long, dark tendrils towards the open chasm. Alice was muttering, over and over, "Sacrifice ... Sacrifice ..."

Bill slipped his pack of cigarettes back under his cap and sneezed. The dust had risen with all the flailing that had been going on.

"So, Lare," he began. The old repairman looked up, his eyes cold blue chips in his sunken face. "Did you come by truck? I mean, have you got your van with you? Equipment?"

Larry nodded.

"Well," said Bill, hitching up his pants as he got to his feet, "since you're up, and if you folks are finished here, I thought we might get started on my renovations. I won't even ask you to charge me a cent." He grinned.

"Larry, what is he saying?" hissed Alice. "What does he want?"

"Just a little hand, Alice, just a little home reno," said Bill, and he chuckled. "You can get dressed first, Lare. Your hairy canary is looking a might cold."

Larry didn't hear him. He was still rooting through the entrails of the chicken and poking at what remained of Mark. "But it's all here, it says so right here!"

The blood began to trickle down into the fissure. Bill frowned, and unconsciously took one step back up onto his stairs.

"The Boundless will rise and—"

What exactly would rise Bill never found out, but he had a fairly good guess. A bulging, hairy arm, too impossibly large for the crack in the floor, punched out of the pit. Clawed fingers wrapped around Mark's dead foot and with a swift jerk the remains slithered down the hole like a broken marionette. Wendy screamed.

The floor rocked as though a giant wheel had turned beneath it. More impossible arms shot out of the fissure, flailing like weird, muscled tentacles amid groans and growls from below. A crack shot up the concrete wall. Wendy jumped up to run, her footfalls heavy as drumbeats. Two of the arms grabbed and hauled her, screaming, backwards into the fiery crevice. The old man was seized around the ankles and pulled to the fissure. He clung to the dirt ledge. Bill had just time enough to see the final look on his face; it was not of rage or fear, but of simple stupefied incredulity—and then he was gone. Larry pleading, shrieking, was next. A hand seized his head, engulfed it, squeezed it, and then yanked; Larry plunged down into the pit in what looked like a poorly executed swan dive. Alice, who had been still throughout all, now shook where she knelt, issuing a steady, lunatic laugh. Spittle ran down her chin and buzzed from her lips. A fine line of drool glinted in the eldritch red light across her chin.

"Alice," Bill said. She did not seem to hear him; he hadn't really expected her to. She caressed one of the massive searching arms and nuzzled it. Without any prompting, she sat down beside the last arm, her legs dangling into the burning pit like a girl taking to the cool waters of the local swimming pool, and she slipped soundlessly in. The last arm disappeared downwards after her.

Bill stayed on the stairs. After counting to sixty, he picked up a rock and tossed it. It hit the dirt and disturbed nothing. They were gone.

Stepping down, Bill collected a portion of the old wire fencing from the corner and unrolled it carefully over the hole, noting with passing interest that there was not a speck of blood or bone from either poor Mark or the poor chicken. He went back to the corner for a couple of cinderblocks. He was able to drag one over, but a sudden needle in his back made him think momentarily that he wouldn't ever be able to stand straight again. One block was enough for now, he decided.

He went back to the steps, noticing again the difference in temperature the moment he was upstairs. Yessir, he would have to get to work first thing in the morning. He would get rid of Larry's truck when he was done, that wouldn't be much of a problem. What *would* be a problem was if Larry didn't have any duct filters. But Bill figured he could get used to the smell, at least for a while, if he needed too. What had happened tonight, while a damn shame, didn't change anything as far as he was concerned.

Although, he would have to find a new gin rummy partner.

***

Evelyn dropped Madeline off two days after Halloween. His sister was madder than a wet hen. Her oldest son had broken his arm after skidding his bike on a patch of sand while turning the last corner home; meanwhile, the youngest had stepped on a nail while playing near a house construction site and would need a tetanus shot. The two boys had hobbled into her home office, holding and dragging their various injuries, at roughly the same moment.

"What kind of mother will they think I am, you little Hell raisers? At the hospital, what will they think!" She slammed the car door and the two boys moaned and bawled and in the backseat.

Bill and the girl waved goodbye and went inside. Madeline watched TV and Bill made her a cup of hot chocolate. He fixed it in a little cup with a saucer for her because he knew how she liked the way they clicked together. He staggered a little while bringing the tray in, and Madeline got up and helped him carry it to the old coffee table.

"Back hurt, Bill?" She never said Uncle Bill except for in front of her mother. She thought it sounded too impressive—which was good for her mother, but not so good for her. Why fancy up something that didn't need fancying? Bill's grimace bunched his big cheeks, but there was a real smile in his eyes.

"Did a little home renovation over the weekend," he said, sitting in his easy chair. "Went a little overboard, but I wanted the job done right."

"The furnace?" she asked, already knowing as she looked at him proudly. Her uncle could do just about anything. "It's really warmer. I like it." They watched the News quietly for a while. She wrinkled her nose.

"But it smells a little bad," she went on, and giggled. "Farty."

"That's sulphur, Mads," he said. "I've got to put in some filters. Didn't have any at the time, but I'm having some delivered and I'll manage until then. But you're right." He cracked a beer and rested back with a sigh in his saggy brown armchair. "It's a helluva stink."

DATE NIGHT

I'm almost ready, you say. It's been a long time since you were ready for anything. It's been a long time since you've said anything.

The evening stirs with impatient but gentle noises: grasses rustling, beetle wings thrumming. The click of a bird swallowing a little water from a chipped rock near your head. Where your head had been.

The night was beautiful, those years ago, and it had not looked away. It was not as the poets say: the sky was not indifferent. Not with those white flashlight beams cutting up through its belly, not with the scream of surprised crickets, leaping from one running pair of feet then another, shivering across its dusky face. You had been laughing, breathless, as you decided the spot

(*Here!*)

never knowing how long you'd stay as you removed your long, cream coat and lay back upon it, one hand nestled beneath your head.

Your smile was lovely, cheeks flushed and happy, and the night glittered in your laughing eyes, touched your curling, golden hair—spread out in the long grass like a bursting star—with long, dark fingers. Curious, the night searched along your sides, raising the little hairs of your arms. Your warm scent (sweat, quick but a little sweet) rose gently, and the night breathed it in, moving the tops of the long grass in a sigh. You hadn't been out of the city in years, you said. Look at all the stars! You'd forgotten how many there were. Turn out the lights, Henry, I want to see them all.

Miles from anywhere, he turned out the lights and the night pressed atop your chest and listened to your heart beating, a soft warm rabbit at home, even as it watched him pick up the rock. You were singing an old song, quietly, when the stars were blocked from your eyes, just for a second as it came down. When the stars glittered there once again, you could no longer see them. You were silent. Your hair was no longer golden. As he walked away, taking your long coat, the night carried your warmth and breathed your scent. He never came back but with every set of the sun, the night returned and held your hands and lay upon your dress as the moths ate your hair and the grass wove you a shawl. You stayed so quiet, and the night waited, as the grasses rose and withered, the snows fell and melted. These things are a shock, no one is ever prepared. But the earth is as kind as it is greedy. The soil drew you safely in, made a room for you, to spread out, to pull together, slowly. The night watched and waited like folded hands, like a beau in a sitting room.

For years.

Years.

Years.

I'm ready.

Your dress is the horizon, your bones hold the sky. The night lowers atop you as the sun sets, presses to your sun-warmed chest, your long golden hair swaying for miles in its cool sigh. You had not forgotten the stars.

LAKEBOTTOM CHARLIE

That water was so cold. We'd been night-swimming at Bridget's Cove before, but September came and took a bite off summer with big, straw-yellow teeth. My muscles felt like clay halfway to the raft; when I pulled myself up, alongside the others, my skin felt rubbery to the touch. Lakes at nighttime are all silver and black, and in the moonlight our skin glistened like trout.

There were five of us: My brother Ian and me; Fern Hendrix, from our street; and two summer kids from the campground. I don't remember their names, but it was one of them who made the dare: Dive down and touch the bottom.

"It's twenty feet down," said Ian, and in speaking unintentionally inviting jeers of "Chicken!" from the summer kids.

Ian stood and looked down at them. We went quiet. My wet ponytail drooped against my neck like a dead leech. The swim-trunks of the summer boys clung to their scrawny legs like old leaves; their eyes were glassy and eager. The wooden raft squeaked on its pontoons under Ian's footfalls. I wanted to tell him he didn't have to, but I also knew that would only embarrass him and he'd do it now no matter what anyone said. He swung his arms and took a deep breath. A summer boy shouted: "Watch out for Charlie!" and Ian said, "What?" and tumbled over the edge, arms pinwheeling, flopping backwards into the lake with a huge splash. We laughed as he surfaced then scrambled back onto the raft, cold water pouring off him.

"Watch for who?"

"Lakebottom Charlie," the summer kid repeated, grinning with teeth like crooked gravestones. "He was a kid who drown here in, like, the 70s or something. They never found the body."

"Bullshit," I said.

"Bull tits," the boy replied, nonsensically. "The guy who owns the campground told me. He said he haunts the bottom of the lake and grabs any kid who disturbs him."

"Your mom grabs any kid," said Fern.

"That's just one of those stories they tell to stop kids from messing around," I said. "It's not true." We all looked at the water.

After a long while, a summer kid said, "Someone go touch the bottom."

No one was laughing now.

"Well, somebody's got to do it."

It seemed to us that somebody did.

Fern turned to the boy. "You go."

The boy wordlessly appealed to each of us; I've never seen anyone look so scared. But we said nothing, and he got to his feet. He was shaking at he slunk to the edge of the raft – but by then we all were. It was so cold: our fingers like brittle bones, our lips like frozen minnows. At the edge, the boy gazed over his shoulder for a last reprieve; we stared back with gallows-spectator sobriety. Given no pardon, he took a deep, wavering breath and dove in. The boy vanished into the black water – but came roaring back up seconds later.

"Cold!"

"Dive down!" we shouted, our nervous reserve bursting, laughter like that frothy cloud of bubbles around him billowing out of us.

"N-no! It's so cold!"

"Dive! Dive!"

He took a thin, bloated-cheek breath and tried to pin-dive straight down from where he feverishly tread, but when he popped back up like a cork he was crying. We made room for him as he scrapped his belly over the edge of the deck and slithered to the middle of the raft. He gulped and looked away as he smeared at his face and tried to pretend to only wipe water.

His friend rubbed his back and then glared at us townies. "Now one of you's guys has to go."

Fern reminded him it was their idea and I said we should forget the whole thing, but Ian got back up. The summer kids looked sullenly up at him. Raft thumping under his feet, Ian strode right to the edge and dove. There was barely a splash, like he'd dived into thick mud. We held our breath for him. Time passed.

"Ian?" I said. The surface of the water was black and still.

One of the summer boys laughed nervously. "How deep did he say it was?"

"Ian?"

It was taking too long. We clung to the edge of the raft, arms bent, noses nearly dipping in the dark water. A minute passed. Then two. The others started calling his name, too, our voices urgent as we slapped and splashed the top of the water like we might guide him up. We all sat straight as something large and white rose from below: A huge belch of bubbles bulged and dissipated in the cold air. Air but no Ian.

I didn't think or consult the others as they started shouting again. I dived.

That summer kid hadn't been lying: The water was freezing deeper below. Stupefyingly cold and the dark consumed the rest of my thoughts. When I opened my eyes, I couldn't see anything, couldn't see my own bubbles. I lost my sense of up. I flipped around, trying to orient myself, my hands flying wide. The knuckles of my left hand scraped through mud, digging up little rocks and weeds. It wasn't as deep as we'd thought; shallow enough to hit your head, dive too hard. I clung to the gritty muck, cutting my fingers but barely able to feel my hands on top of not being able to see them. So, I don't know how I saw him just then in that dark, but I did.

A pale form floating face down, turning slowly, rolled on a soft current. His dark hair floating like weeds, his face a blur of deathly white. One ghostly arm drifted out as if searching for a way out of there, for up, out, and air. His face turned my way ... But I was out of breath. A cough warbled from my lips as my lungs tugged for air. Muddy water burned my nose as I inhaled. I sank my toes into the mud and pushed off, pumping my legs like mad, clawing at the water above me. I could hear the others, still yelling, their voices warped and watery like a drown radio.

I burst through the surface. "He's there!"

I coughed out water and gasped. The cold air burned. My mumbling numb lips worked to get the words out. "Directly b-below me. I think he hit his head ..."

I stopped talking, confused by the sounds above. They weren't screaming; they were laughing.

Ian stood triumphant in the middle of the group, grinning like a jack-o'-lantern, freckles like black stars against his moonlit skin, his eyes an uneasy mix of pride and apology.

"There's an air pocket under the raft!" one of the summer kids was hooting. "This dumbass was just letting us freak out."

The water at my toes grew colder.

"I saw you."

"Sorry, Claire," said Ian.

A cold hand gently wrapped around my ankle.

I kicked, a rooster tail of water exploding behind me as I swam for land. I heard Ian shout my name, someone else yell, "It was a joke!" But their voices trailed away, replaced suddenly by screams.

I didn't look back, couldn't. When I could touch land, I put my feet down and smashed the lake out of my way as I ran, the water bursting around my legs until it was shallow enough and my feet carried me out like a duck taking flight. I heard two frenzied dives, could hear the kicking and shouting. I looked around but could not see who was who in the dark and white-churned water. I hoped on the spot, wanting to run but unable to leave. Ian was soon crawl-running out of the shallows and I was done waiting. I grabbed his arm, pulled him up, and we ran for home. On the road back to town, Fern caught up to us. The road wound through the trees and around the water's edge and I could still hear screaming. Or were they laughing? Were they playing in the water, all to themselves now that they'd scared the townies off? Yes, I wanted to say that they were laughing; that they'd made up that story, that they'd had a third friend swim out from the side of the lake and dive down, that it was a prank, and we hadn't just abandoned them. I wanted to say that then but I didn't say anything as road turned to street, just puffed and shivered under streetlights, no towels, bare feet sore on the asphalt.

I never saw those summer kids again, but they come and go, don't they? And I've never been back to Bridget's Cove. At least, not at night. The water is too cold.

MINE IS NOT

The demon looked like the girl, but the girl looked dead. Father Brennan hoped she was not, that this was a trick of the Adversary, and that by the Grace of God all would be well. He had not returned to the room upstairs—with its slowly pulsing walls and sputtering candles—since his first encounter two days earlier and had no interest in going back in alone. He'd made the phone call after what happened to the dog. Now, he sat waiting on a hardback chair in the front hall, hands cupping his arthritic knees, sweat itching at his starched collar, and checking the grandfather clock every few seconds like a nervous date. They were late.

The rest of the family waited and wept in the living room. Five in total: mother, father, two brothers, and grandmother. He could see the grandmother from where he sat, mouth puckered like a cat's ass, glaring at him through tinted bifocals. She had disapproved of his being there, thought the whole thing was bunk. The girl was just being dramatic, she'd said. Just needed a good whup. Father Brennan looked down at his bandaged hand, blood blushing through the cotton folds. If this was drama, it was the most ungodly performance he'd ever seen.

The front door opened. The priest stood; in the living room the family started, the youngest giving a faint cry.

"Hello?" A man knocked on the open portal and let himself the rest of the way in. He might have been on his way to a rock concert, tight pants, slick hair, aviator sunglasses. "Anybody home?"

A small woman, his wife and not nearly as flashy, followed behind, swinging a rosary and muttering rapidly.

Father Brennan extended his uninjured hand and took a step forward. "Thank you for coming on such short—"

The man suddenly dropped to one knee, head bent, and hands clasped; his wife closed her eyes and held her palms up like a set of empty scales.

"Thank you, oh Lord, for delivering us to this family in their time of crisis," the man said loudly. "Though we are not worthy, we will be the vectors of your mighty and righteous justice."

His wife groaned, "Amen."

The man got to his feet. "Alan Torrence, Demonologist," he said. "This is my wife, Malba."

"Thank you for coming on such short—"

"We've been knocking for some time," said Alan, whipping off his sunglasses and tucking them into his breast pocket. "No answer."

The priest shook his head. "I'm sorry, I didn't hear you."

"The force here does wish to be heard," murmured his wife.

"I heard you," said the grandmother. Her son and daughter-in-law looked tired; the kids giggled nervously. "And I hoped you'd leave. This is all bunk."

"Mom, that's enough," said the young father on the couch, arms wrapped around his two boys.

Alan did not go in to greet the family but tilted his chiselled jaw towards the stairs. "Show me the girl."

***

A two weeks earlier, the oldest Pritchett daughter, Nellie, had gone to a party. She had come home late, smelling like cigarettes, but otherwise fine. She had filled a glass of water from the kitchen tap, said goodnight to her mother and father (who had been waiting up, watching TV), and gone to bed. Her parent's had agreed that she might have had a beer, but at sixteen they figured that was pretty responsible and they were proud of their daughter. There was a lot to be proud of: good grades, a team player, helped out around the house. One little beer at an end of year party was nothing. They went to bed safe in the knowledge that all was well in the parenting department and dreamed easily.

In the morning, Nellie couldn't get out of bed. She missed the bus and when her father came in to check on her before he left for work, he asked, sorely disappointed, what she had taken. She said nothing. He didn't believe her and left her to marinade in her misery. By the time he and his wife returned home from work, Nellie looked like an addict in the worst stages of withdrawal, groaning and writhing, sweating so profusely they had to lay garbage bags under her sheets. By that evening, she was filling buckets with vomit, screaming as she dry-heaved on acid, and they finally bundled her into the car. At the hospital, she was put on drips to rehydrate, hooked up to every machine, run through every test. No doctor could tell them what was wrong, what was happening. By the small hours, the bleeding began. From every orifice, from under her fingernails, between the follicles of her hair. Nellie screamed like a woman on fire as she became a slick crimson pillar and her parents were dragged, frantic, from her room. The monitors panicked and flashed; the crash team shouted commands around her bed. No one on staff had ever seen anything like it; more than one would not go near her, afraid it was catching. A single kind nurse took Mister and Missus Pritchett aside in the hallway and told to them to be brave: One way or another, it would be over soon.

By morning, it was done.

Nellie sat in her bed, freshly washed, cleanly dressed in hospital attire, crusts of blood drying in the corners of her eyes and under her nailbeds, regarding the world from behind sallow, almost translucent skin. Her parents had been allowed back in, and her mother scooped her into her arms not minding the cold, clammy touch of her daughter's skin, heedless of the phlegmy rumble deep in her daughter's chest: she was alive. Alive, alive, alive.

Nellie stayed at the hospital for another three days for observation. Her vitals remained normal, and she never again experienced any of the first night's symptoms—although she continued to look sickly, physically was weak, and her skin remained chill and rubbery. No explanation could be made for what the condition had been or what had brought it on. She was sent home to applause from nurses and visiting friends, never speaking a word, her flat affect never shifting.

That night, her mother dug several blade steaks out of the freezer and after a quick nuke in the microwave began to fry them up with onion and mushrooms. The doctor's had told her that Nellie would need iron. Mrs. Pritchett had left the kitchen to get the bag of potatoes from the cold-room, and when she returned found Nellie standing over the stove, half a bloody steak crammed in her mouth, the juices and sizzling pan grease running down her chin and neck, down into her sweater. Nellie looked around at her mother with bloodshot eyes and without looking away effortlessly bit the steak in half and swallowed the slab in several, choking gulps. Mrs. Pritchett stood at the cold-room door, clutching the bag of potatoes to her chest, her breath catching in her throat. Nellie twisted one hand around the heavy iron skillet's hot handle and, turning, took the whole thing with her out of the kitchen. Mrs. Pritchett followed at a distance, watched her daughter plod up the stairs, listened to the creak of the hall floor above, and the door to Nellie's bedroom open and slam shut.

***

"She hasn't left the room since."

Father Brennan and the Torrence's stood at the top of the stairs. Nellie's room was at the very end of the carpeted hallway, staring back at them with a silence that seemed hateful.

"They brought her food, but now are too afraid. Since the dog and the ... changes," the priest explained. "She doesn't try to leave, at least she hasn't tried yet." He retrieved a handkerchief from his sleeve and daubed at his glistening forehead. "The Pritchett's aren't religious, but still they called me."

"Trying times makes seers of sinners," intoned Alan, hands on hips, legs slightly spread in a gunslinger's stance.

"I've done what I can," Father Brennan went on, haltingly, "I've sent word to my bishop for the exorcism, but the Church is hesitant to reach that option. It takes time, assessments ... But I don't know that we have time. I knew you were just a few hours away, so I called ... The bishop has no idea."

"Father, you did the right thing," said Alan, clapping a hand on the older man's shoulder. He was trembling badly. "We've rumbled with this type before, dozens of them, and no matter how ugly it gets we've got the light of the Divine on our side. We'll go in alone, get a feel for this sucker. We'll call you when we need you."

The priest began to protest—but stopped and instead nodded, thankfully.

The couple joined hands, recited a prayer, and approached the door together. The wriggling tips of purple veins growing between the door and the frame gave them pause, but they cracked like brittle roots as the Torrences thrust the door open.

The room was not a room.

Every surface—the floor, bed, windows, walls—was sheeted with a soft lavender and crimson membrane, twisting and muscular, like the interior lining of a stomach. It smelled of rot but pulsed gently. The candles brought earlier by the priest provided the only light; most of them were nearly drown in their own wax, and the room was dark as a snake's mouth beyond these feeble halos. Alan stepped back, nearly turned to run, but Malba grasped his wrist and held him fast.

"Ours is a God of miracles and might," she whispered firmly, wrapping her rosary tight about her hand. She entered the room with her head held high. Alan followed and the door closed behind them.

The girl was crouched on a mound in the corner that might have once been a dresser. She glanced up at the sound of the latch clicking but otherwise was uninterested and went back to work. She was naked except a for a long t-shirt, her hair hanging lank and unwashed across her shoulders. She was bloody from toe to knee, finger to elbow, from days of walking, crouching, and working in her membranous chamber. Clutched in one hand was a long sharp bone with bits of grey fur and sinew still attached. She used it like a stylus to scratch symbols, over and over, into the meaty walls.

With trembling hands, Alan pulled out a small Bible from his inner coat pocket and began to read, stammering at first but gaining confidence with each familiar passage. His voice grew, raising to a stage performers projection as he finished the lines, reached for his holy water, and raised it over his head. A cracking sound interrupted the ritual. Alan looked up. The girl, the demon, was biting down on the end of the bone, snapping the end to a sharper point with her teeth. The girl's own teeth were long-since shattered; stronger, longer teeth shifted in her jaw from beneath.

Malba and Alan met each other's eyes and Alan started again, in Latin this time. Malba got down onto her knees and began to pray from the floor, making the sign on the cross, rocking back and forth, and calling upon every saint, angle, and principality of Heaven to assist them in their work. The demon looked around, seeming to recognize some of the ancient words as Alan spoke, but soon lost interest and climbed down from the mound to scratch at the floor with its stylus.

Alan began to sweat, frustration overtaking his fear, and once more he raised his holy water and this time flung it at the demon. "In the name of God Almighty! In the name of the Father, and the Son—"

The water splashed across the demon's work, wetting the mucous that rose from the floor and streaking the symbol. The demon spun where it crouched, finally taking interest, its mouth dropping to its chest, splitting the girl's ashen flesh to the ears. It roared. Alan's moment of triumph flashed and died like a flare in the sky as the demon twisted its hands and rent open the floor, violently serrating the fleshy ground. The membranes beneath thrashed and whipped, clapping shut suddenly over Malba before she could react or make a sound, her mass quickly consumed, dissolved, and incorporated into the tissues of the pulsing room. Alan began to scream, faster and faster until he lost all sense.

Father Brennan burst into the room as Alan too disappeared beneath the folds of the room, his screams unending, the walls livid. The demon turned its rotting face to the old priest and to the open hallway beyond. Brennan stumbled backwards as the thing tilted its head and strode forward, words spilling from the old man's papery lips as he held his crucifix forward like a rapier. The demon did not slow.

"I send you back to the Pit! In the name of God," he said, retreating to the hallway, voice rising to a shriek, becoming frenzied. "Mine is the Christian God! And He—"

The demon wrapped a hand about the old priest's throat. Teeth like rusted nails tore the girl's lips apart as a boggy, grating voice spoke from deep in its chest.

"Mine is not."

YELLOW BIRDS

I first saw the birds in the field where the witches were buried. Four little birds, no bigger than sparrows, each a different shade of yellow: amanita, sulphur, laburnum, and gold. Glass from a beer bottle had ripped up my bicycle's front tire and I had to stop. A drunk must have tossed the bottle. I hate the drunks. They killed my cat, Mary, last October because she was black and there. I held a funeral for her under the row of lilac bushes where she had liked to sleep. The old shovel I used to dig the grave was so heavy and the handle gave me splinters. Mom got angry because I'd dug too close to the lilac roots; I got angry because my cat was dead.

I can't stand the smell of lilacs now.

The day I saw the birds was grey and cold, even for Spring. The farmers were burning their fields and on either side of the road the ground was scabby and black or smouldering. But not the witch field. No one in their right mind would plant anything there.

None of the kids I used to see when I went into town with mom or at summer activities had ever been in the field. There was nothing there for a regular kid to see or do: no plaque to deface, no stones to overturn, no memorial to waste rolls of toilet paper on at Halloween. I know because I went into the field once, after Mary died, driving mom's little car (seat pushed back and standing, halting between gas and break) and since then I've always looked to the something that isn't there whenever I ride my bike past.

I guess the birds must have known that.

The long grass was dull and still flat from rain and my birds stood out like gems on unwashed hair. The lone, lightning-struck tree at the center (where the witches had been hanged) looked particularly arresting. The colours were all right together and I wished that I was good at painting so that I could keep the scene in my room, hang it over my bed to look at when I slept. I'm not good at painting, but I am very good at other things. Identifying weaknesses, for example. Even in myself. It is one of my greatest strengths.

The birds stayed as they were while I walked my bike with its ruined tire (not just popped but bent from falling) into the ditch and laid it down, hiding it from the road, from the drunks. I stared back at them when I stood, thinking they would fly away first, but they weren't like birds that way. I picked up the small bag of groceries I'd been carrying. They were very still, no twists of the heads or nervous hops on the wet hay. Have you ever seen a bird sit perfectly still and unafraid? I took some running steps at them and when they didn't move, I turned around and kept going down the road, walking. I've never owned a cell phone, and anyway I could not call my mom for a ride. I would walk home, get a spare tire off of one of the other bikes in the garden shed, and walk back to fix my broken one. It would be longer but easier than struggling all the way home with my broken bike and the groceries.

Problem solving is another one of my strengths.

The corner of the milk was leaking and beginning to soak everything else by the time I got home. It was almost dark and I wished that I'd remembered to leave a light on inside. Our house is not as old as it looks, only from the seventies, and is built well and made to be self-reliant. My father always said a house had to rely on itself. There are no neighbours, which I like. The only things outside are lawns, trees, and then fields. And the lilac bush, but I don't like that. The biggest lawn is devoted to a huge vegetable garden, and I've been sowing it, weeding it, harvesting it, and laying it to rest again for the winter since I was five. The stove is wood burning, and there are trees all around, so as long as you remember to cut them often and let the wood season for about six months, you're fine. Our axe is not as heavy as the old shovel, and we have a wood splitter in the basement that's so easy to use a kid half my age could figure it out. I was born here, homeschooled here, and have I've lived here my whole life—which you may not think is impressive because of my age, but it's all I've got.

I was making a mental note to always leave the living room light on, the screen door still open and in my hand, when I saw the birds sitting on my old swing set. Birds can fly faster than a person can walk, so it didn't surprise me that they might get there before me. What did surprise me was that my bike was leaning against rusted metal slide. Both tires were full and round. I let the screen door crash back into place, but my birds didn't startle or move at my approach, they just stared, their ink-drop eyes like tiny holes in the back of the world.

I didn't make it to the swing set, but at least I didn't run back to the door. The bike stayed out there overnight, and the birds were gone by morning. But I didn't trust it; I knew they were nearby. It worried me that someone would come by and see the bike propped there and think I'm irresponsible without even knowing it, but I wouldn't touch it. Days passed and I needed go to for groceries again. I was so worried that I almost couldn't remember if I went to Winston's country store or Black's convenience store last time I went shopping. I didn't like to repeat myself. I know it's okay to be worried as long as you do something about it, but it still felt bad to worry. I'd left the bike in that field, and now it was back and just fine.

I wondered what else might come back.

***

I finally remembered it was Winston's I had been to and so I fixed up mom's old bike and headed to Black's when I ran out of bread. I also needed more jam, canned vegetables, toothpaste, and of course milk. I'd bought seeds in March and had started them already in the living room in the cardboard egg cartons I'd saved all winter, so I hoped soon I wouldn't have to buy canned food anymore. I also needed to go to the library to return my books and the DVD I'd borrowed. It's not a real library, but a library outpost in the post office basement and only accessible by a door next to the dumpster for the only coffee shop in town. The outpost is occasionally overseen by an old man, but most days he doesn't oversee anything, just sits in a folding chair beside the dumpster picking a dented guitar and feeding the stray cats that hang around. He's not responsible at all but in this case I don't mind. It's all self-check out, anyway, and he always smiles and never says hello when I see him. I appreciate that.

Black's is never busy during the daytime, but I'm always careful to go only after two o'clock: it is earlier than public school is out but not so early to raise any uncomfortable questions about a homeschooler, like me.

I was almost finished when I heard my name. I didn't want to turn around but when someone says your name, they hold you with it.

"Hey there, Kitty. Doing some errands for you mom?"

I smiled up at the man. "Hello." Smiling little girls are easy to forget.

Jim Sturges, who used to be my dad's friend before my dad died in an ATV accident, set a case of beer on the counter. I didn't say his name; I wanted him to leave.

"How's your mom?"

"Fine."

"House holding up okay?"

"I take care of it."

"I know you do."

He'd lost a lot of weight since the days he and dad would go camping, ATVing, or just sit and smoke out back. It'd been almost five years since I'd seen him. But except for the waddle of loose skin under his stubbly chin, and the red hang-dog expression of his watery eyes, he looked mostly the same. A look of concern passed over his face.

"I haven't seen your mom around much lately," he said.

I almost said, "She hasn't seen you around, either," but stopped. My birds, all of a sudden lined up on the crossbar to the front door, had distracted me in time. It was a mysterious thing to say, and people wanted to solve mysteries.

"I'll tell her," I said instead, and I knew this was the right thing to say because he was already forgetting me, slipping his debit card into the machine, chatting with the woman behind the counter, passing his conversation from me to her. I slipped my shopping bag over my shoulder and headed to the door. My birds were gone.

At the library, the old man was at his right place at the counter of the library outpost, not playing guitar. I saw the book I wanted on the front display but dropped off my books and DVD without asking for it and left.

Returning home from the library, the (amanita, sulphur, lemon, and gold) yellow birds were all waiting in a row. Beside them on the porch rail was the book, the very one I would have taken from the library if I had stayed long enough to choose. It sat there, like the bike, a little gift. The birds watched me. *See what we can bring you, bring back for you?* There are things I want, things I want back. But I never meant to give the birds anything.

***

Things were not okay after dad died. Mom used to be so responsible, but after the accident she couldn't get out of bed, she'd get angry and stay angry, she'd drink. Running a house for one is not too bad; running a house for two when one wants things a certain way, but that way is gone, is impossible.

At first at least there were casseroles, more than I knew what to do with. I didn't have to think about shopping and food then, but that summer the garden suffered and I realised that you had to think about things, remember things, even when you don't want to. All mom wanted to do was forget. She successfully forgot in several ways. Old friends stopped coming around, and new friends would stay too long. Dad used to say the house took care of itself, but there is a schedule to keep in a self-sufficient house: a time when wood must be cut and rotated, when seeds must go into the ground if you want the plants to come back. Mom didn't have to work any more after the money from dad's insurance came in. She didn't fully trust banks and she put a lot of it in coffee cans down in the basement next to the unassuming preserved pickles and cherries. The rest she showed me was all online, in a chequing account she'd had open since she was just a little older than me. She showed me to reassure me, she said, that we were all right. But she also showed me where the bill payments came from—just in case she happened to forget. It wasn't good to be owing, she said. But if you owe, you pay up. Sometimes I go to the bank now and put a little in, just to top it up again for the bills.

It's amazing what you can do by yourself these days.

It's a steady rule in life—for banks, for gardens, for effort—that you've got to put a little something in if you want to take something out again. You have to put a lot more in if you want to take something out completely.

***

The witches were hanged on the last day of September, 1676. Our town is so small—a village really—that it's been able to keep that information to itself, mostly. Salem is famous for its witch trials, but here there was no trial. Because our witches were real.

A camp of fur trappers went missing and screams were heard from the woods for months afterwards, babies were stolen up chimneys, and wives normally happy at home would walk out into the trees, cradling the still warm spine of their husband, never to be seen again.

Catching an actual witch is a hard thing, killing them is even harder. No one is really sure how they did it anymore, but the night they hanged them, the tree from which they were dropped was struck five times with lightning. It burned but never fell and has stood the same way since.

I saw the tree up close the day after I'd tried to bury Mary. I had wanted some place special, and the lilac bush already belonged to Mary. I was still angry at mom, even though I shouldn't have been. Anger is so much easier to deal with than fear, or sadness, or regret, or panic. The tree was like a great stone arm, rising out of the ground, five fingers cradling the setting sun. I dug with my hands, looking up and around mom's parked car towards the road, checking that no one was there, no one was watching. Part of me wanted someone to see me, to stop me, and to punish me. But no one came by, and no one saw. The earth below it was soft, ready to receive and to take away. I didn't even need a shovel—which was good, because ours was broken now.

***

It's the end of summer now, and my bike is still leaning on the old swing set, rusted and stiff from neglect. The library book sits on the porch railing, fat, mildewed, and swollen with rain and damp. I have not been back to the library in case the old man thinks I stole it and let it get ruined. I don't go to the store anymore in case there are people I might be warned against talking to—which is a kind of gift, too. And I don't want to take any of their gifts. There are other gifts around the yard that I am too responsible to touch: the clothes that fell off the line one day and stayed clean for a day, the fresh can of gas for the empty lawnmower. The grass has grown long and yellow; I don't have time to play there, anyway. The garden grew, too, but because I wanted it to. I will have to harvest early. There are only cans of money down in the cellar now. I ran out of shampoo and soap a while ago, but that is okay. I cut my hair all off so I didn't have to worry about it being so dirty. Dishes are harder to wash, so I've just stopped using them.

I am in the garden, digging out a carrot with the back of our little axe, when I see the fluttering yellow and my heart leaps thinking my birds have finally flown away, will stop leaving gifts so I can get back to being responsible. It sinks just as quickly when I realise they are flying. I have never seen them fly before, never seen them move. They are moving quickly towards me, down the road, clouded in a storm of dust.

It is very clever of them. I have rejected their gifts, their bribes, and so now they have disguised themselves as lights. The four yellow front lights of an ATV coming now to make me accept the gifts, so that I will owe them, will have to plant something else at the base of the lightning-struck tree in return to balance the books. I keep my axe in my hand and crouch behind the lilac bush. The flowers are dead but the leaves are full.

The ATV stops on the other side of the lilac bush, the grunting engine rumbles to a soft plinking as Jim swings himself off the old, cracked seat. The same seat my dad flew straight off when they'd been horsing around, trying to jump a ditch, or some other stupid drunk way to die.

"Jesus." Jim's voice is low. I can see him gazing around the overgrown lawn, to the dark windows of the house, to the lawnmower and bike rusting into the long grass. He cups his hands to the sides of his mouth and calls, "Shauna? Kitty?"

I don't reply, but hold my axe tight in both hands, my chin resting on the butt-end. His footsteps are very loud on the gravel of our driveway. I peer around the edge of the lilac. And there are my birds, two on the ATV handlebars, two on Jim's head. He hasn't noticed a thing and I have to hold in a giggle, how silly he looks. Then it occurs to me. It was my dad's ATV, and mom had no right giving it away. I could go to the store again with it, the next town over, and no one would even notice me. I could put my groceries in the hatch under the seat. I could drive through the fields instead of on the roads. It's not really a gift, it's mine. The birds are only making that clear. And if I gave them just one more thing, maybe they'll bring just one more thing back. The thing I want back most.

The grass is soft and quiet under my bare feet, Jim cannot hear me over his own boots. The birds on his head do not move and I don't want to hit them. He's walking ahead of me, so I get him to stop, hold him with his own name. He is surprised to see me. My mother used to say I was full of surprises.

It is one of my greatest strengths.

ON THE PALE ROAD HOME

On the road, the snow is blinding. The snowfall hadn't looked so serious at the warm, garland-festooned doorstep of Tristan's house, the cheerful mumble of mulled conversation and winter-spiced laughter wrapping playfully around her shoulders.

"Call a cab," Tristan had said.

"Less than a mile to my house," she'd insisted. "It'll take longer just waiting for it."

Staggering only slightly down the driveway, waving over her shoulder as she went, she'd headed for the streetlight up the road. Now, standing beneath the streetlight's gauzy glow, she wonders if she should head back, finish another conversation and glass of wine. She looks around for the driveway, holding her hat on her head.

"Hey!"

A woman appears, running, from out of the confusion of snow. Her eyes are lively with drink. "Care to escort a lady home?"

She doesn't recognize her, but she could have only come from the party.

They start walking down the dark road, leaving the silvery blush of the streetlight. Two blurs side-by-side in comfortable silence. The world behind and between the incessant snow is black—but the road, the road is a pale rib stuck in the dark throat of the woods. The blowing snow tucks their tracks back beneath their toes with every step. She is glad she decided to walk. Driving conditions would be terrible.

"We should cross," she says. The snow and wind dull her voice. They are on the wrong side of the road for walking, and she says so. "We'll see the headlights coming, safer that way."

They cross.

"Good thinking," says the other woman, her own voice raised. "Not like we're dressed for visibility." The other woman points to her own white peacoat, then to her black jacket. After a moment of silence, she adds. "You know, there's supposed to be a ghost on this road. A woman killed while walking home alone one night."

"Hit by a car?"

She shrugs. "Don't know. Just that she walks the road and guides people home." She laughs. "Maybe she's you."

"Maybe she's you."

"I think I'd know."

"Would you?"

The crunch of their boots is barely audible above the wind. She can feel the snow piling on her head, melting on her cheeks, and the way the other woman keeps glancing over. The silly thing has scared herself with her own ghost story. And she isn't wearing much: No hat, heeled boots, bare hands pushed into the small pockets of her trim, white peacoat.

"Aren't you cold?"

The other woman shakes her head. "I don't get cold very easily."

"I'm always cold."

"Can't seem to get warm?"

They each stare ahead and walk in silence.

You would know, she thinks. *You would know if you were dead. Life demands you know the difference.*

"Do you live nearby?"

The other woman doesn't reply. Silly thing, probably freezing. The world is very dark now, the first streetlight far behind, the next too far to see. But all she has to do is keep walking, keep walking in this direction and she'll be home soon. Her thoughts keep circling back. *Surely you could tell for yourself, such a reality did not depend on the opinion of another. Especially someone who didn't know better than not to dress for the cold. Or to walk home alone in the dark.*

"I must almost be home," she says just to say something.

The soft glow of another streetlight blooms lazily through the swirling snow. Thoughts seem to fade as the world grows more distinctly blurred with snow, falling faster than before. She sighs a foggy, wind-stolen breath—only to find herself alone. She looks back.

The woman is several scared steps back, her features erased by shadow and snow.

She has no face.

Then she is gone, her white coat snapping behind her, as she runs fast down a narrow side road, perhaps a driveway. In seconds, it is like she was never there.

You would know, she thinks into the swirling night. And then, *I must almost be home.* Eyes full of snow, she looks back down the dark, endless road. Driving conditions will be terrible. It is good she walked.

Someone approaches alone from the dark beyond the snow. They are on the wrong side of the road. She should tell them, guide them to this side. She is almost home; she will just do this one favour. She crosses over.

RECIPE CARDS OF MISS GRACE PROCKTOR, WITH NOTES

June 11th 1957
Lemon Blueberry Cake

Ingredients: Butter, desiccated coconut, caster sugar, flour, eggs (large), vanilla, finely grated zest of lemon, frozen wild blueberries (picked by hand, in the evening), salt.

Preheat oven to 350F

Grease 9x10" springform pan. In a medium bowl mix coconut, sugar, flour, and salt. Whisk to cure of lumps.

Whisk eggs in separate bowl. Add butter, vanilla, and lemon zest. Blend well and combine with dry mix.

Fold in blueberries. Pour into pan. Tap to remove bubbles from the heart.

Bake until toothpick can be cleanly removed.

Will keep on shelf three days; freezes well.

Notes: A success! Makes an excellent morning or evening cake. Big hit at Anne's garden lunch. Jimmy Vincent had thirds. I promised him I'd make another just for him. Cake was sweeter with tea this evening.

August 16th 1957
Dry-Rubbed Ribs with Apple Chutney

Ingredients, Dry Rub: Paprika, brown sugar, pepper, salt, garlic, onion

Ingredients, Glaze: Vinegar, tomato paste, salt, pepper, honey

Ingredients, Chutney: 2 firm red apples, fresh mint (chopped), mustard (hot), maple syrup, oil, vinegar, salt to taste.

Ribs: 1 rack, membrane carefully removed

Preheat oven to 250F

Combine dry rub ingredients. Massage into meat (get into the cracks and folds, do not be shy). Secure in tin foil, bake for three hours. Combine glaze and make chutney as you wait.

Chop apple finely, do not be afraid of the skin. Mix all other ingredients into a small, clean mason jar, shake vigorously. Pour over chopped apple, set aside.

Remove ribs, allow to cool. Remove the bones. They should slide out cleanly in your fingers. Reserve bones for soup.

Apply glaze. Broil on high for 5 minutes.

Notes: One of Jimmy's favourites. The secret is in the mint. It must be picked when young by moonlight. Silver sheers provide the most favourable cut. Flavours balance well and develop overnight. Made extra and into sandwiches for Jimmy's card table; already getting request for the recipe for their wives. Will make myself unpopular at next bridge game with this one. Might share with Anne the recipe; she can keep a secret. A good friend as culinary confidante is worth their weight in saffron.

October 17th 1957
Apple Crumble

Ingredients: Apples (peeled, sliced, cored), white sugar, brown sugar, flour, oats, baking powder, baking soda, cinnamon, water, butter (melted)

Preheat oven 350F

Prepare the apples. Do not be sluttish; they should be clean, neat, and even for best quality and results. Reserve the skin for jams. Arrange apple slices into a 9x12" pan.

Mix white sugar, a drop of flour, and cinnamon together. Sprinkle over the arranged apple slices.

Mix oats, flour, baking powder and soda, brown sugar, and butter until coarse, like loose soil.

Crumble over all.

Bake 45 minutes.

Notes: ~~A beautiful fall dish. Classic and simple. Great compliment to any meal and always popular. Nothing smells better when baking.~~

He said the apples were sour. I know this is not true. The hill by which I picked them was generous and cold, the same as last month. Nothing was taken that should not have been; I am very careful. Not sure what went wrong (butter gone off?) Cannot eat entire pan by myself. Brought the rest to Anne, but she had already made one of her own that morning.

January 21st 1958
Cream of Celery Soup

Ingredients: Butter, small onion (finely chopped), celery (finely chopped), garlic clove (large), flour, chicken broth, whole milk, salt, pepper.

Melt the butter in large saucepan. Cook celery, onion, and garlic until soft, almost translucent. Add flour, brown lightly. Add broth and milk, stir until smooth.

Increase the heat, bring to a simmer, and reduce to low. Add remaining ingredients.

It may simmer on low for an awfully long time.

To remove lumps, add cup by cup to a blender. Ensure blades are sharp. Mix it well.

May be enjoyed immediately or at leisure, bowl by bowl. Freezes well.

Notes: A comforting soup when all alone. Can be enjoyed as part of a meal or on its own. Rich but fresh in the winter months. Not so much work that it cannot be made for solitary dining. Better than any tin from the store.

June 17th 1958
White Cake with Buttercream Icing (for celebrations)

Ingredients, Cake: Flour, baking powder, salt, sugar, oil, eggs, rosewater, vanilla

Ingredients, Icing: Confectioners sugar, butter (softened), vanilla, milk

Preheat oven 325F

Sift dry ingredients into large bowl. Combine sugar, oil, eggs in separate bowl. Add to dry and mix well.

Bake 45 minutes.

Mix icing ingredients into large bowl and mix with an electric beater. Do not overmix, or the butter will weep.

Remove cake from oven. Once cake has cooled, remove from pans. Level if necessary. Liberally frost cakes.

Decorate with anything you have on hand: Flowers, picks, toppers.

Note: It is a compliment when your cooking is so well-regarded that you are asked by friends for a special confection for a special occasion, like a wedding or a birth. You ought to be flattered to be included so intimately on such an important occasion, to fold your own fortunes and distinct care into the preparations. The recipe is so simple, you may wish to add your own ingredients. The key is to be subtle, but not too subtle. Every cook has her own methods; I will not expose mine.

November 3rd 1959
Hasenpfeffer

Ingredients, Marinade: Water, red wine, vinegar, salt, rosemary, juniper berries (crushed), black pepper, bay leaves, cloves, thyme.

Ingredients, Meat: Rabbit (or hare) portioned to legs and breasts (reserve and grind remaining bones), butter, flour, onion.

Combine marinade in pot bring to boil. Remove from heat, allow to cool. Submerge meat. Cover and let sit overnight.

Remove meat, pat dry. It will appear quite red. Dredge in flour, heat butter in skillet, brown the meat. Remove and set aside.

Deglaze skillet with red wine. Add more butter, cook onions until brown.

Return rabbit to pan. Add reserved marinade. You MUST bring briefly to a rolling boil or it will not cook. Cover, place in oven.

Cook 2-4 hours for wild hare; 1-2 hours for house rabbit.

Notes: A German dish with an intimidating name, but don't be frightened. Originally a ragout from the blood and innards and less appreciated pieces of the animal, discarded and thought unsuitable for other dishes. Though much game could formerly make a Pfeffer (boar, deer) young rabbit is best. They are leaner in the winter, but also hungrier and easier to catch. To snare your own is the finest thing. Do not let it suffer; it sours the meat. Do not be alarmed by the sounds they make; it's not unlike a child crying.

Be sure to reassure any neighbours you might encounter; sound can carry quite far over the cold snow. Cut below the jaw, hang to drain, reserve the blood; there is always a use for young blood. Cut off the feet (they bring no luck, discard) and remove the skin in one gentle pull, like a silk stocking.

A rich, savoury dish to wow any guest on any occasion, be it a merry dinner party between friends. Or a more somber occasion.

Should guests ask: *Hassen*: to hate. *Hase*: a hare. It is easy to confuse as it rolls off the tongue.

February 19th 1960
Brown Bread

Ingredients: Boiling water, oats, butter, molasses, flour, fresh ground fine powder, yeast, salt.

Important. Grind bones, sparingly mixed with flour. Any bones will do. If you do not have any to spare, consult an old friend. Perhaps she will provide you with what you need.

In a large bowl, pour the boiling water over the oats Stir in butter and molasses, let stand.

In separate bowl, combine bone flour, yeast, and salt.

Add to oats and blend.

Turn onto a floured surface; knead until smooth and elastic.

Well-worked dough has a way of crying out, gasping with bubbles and refusing to remain friendly. Work until it relents.

Place in a greased bowl, cover with a clean cloth, and allow to rise in a warm place for one hour or until doubled in size.

Punch it down.

Divide and shape into loaves. Place in two 9x5" pans, let rise.

Preheat oven to 375F.

Bake 40 minutes.

Notes: Is there anything more comforting to a lonely home than freshly baked bread? And the bachelor or widower in your neighbourhood will always appreciate this thoughtful gift. Wrap it in a clean, white cloth and deliver it warm. Or, if you are at liberty, make yourself at home in their kitchen and prepare on-site.

Few will turn you out—but remember closely if they do.

WE ARE GIANTS

When I was young, I would walk the fields behind my house. Often alone, I observed my father's warnings about coyotes—although the only coyote I knew was a cunning inventor, bumbling but not a villain, and had no plans for solitary children. That was the wolf's job. There were cows in the field, and I would watch the herd quietly, their slow-moving swagger, their placid glances. I would name any one of them that came within arms-reach Buttercup. I would listen to their rumbling, throaty basses as the dusk choir of predators beyond the trees provided melody. I was not afraid, but I always went home before dark.

Walking with my father the fields became bigger, safer. Iron skies felt protective and only brightened the blooming daisies, yellow cowslips, and pink apple blossoms yet undiscovered by the plodding cattle. I would pluck the stems or snap the blooming twigs from gnarled trees and tuck the flowers decoratively behind an ear, imagining that the tantalizing burst of gold proudly displayed in my long dark hair would lure a Buttercup close enough to tame. It was patience, dad would say, and gentleness that would bring them close. My mother had taught me to be patient, and I could be gentle if I wanted. They are all gone now, but when I remember back I remember the cows first. I would try to feed the large brown beasts some of the green bean pods dad always kept in his pockets as he told me again the story of how his great, great grandfather had started the herd after selling his last cow for a pittance and then setting off to find his fortune.

I learned not to ask what happened after the happy ending.

***

Winter was always harder. Years before I was born, my mother had immigrated to Canada from a country closer to the sun (*so she'd say*) before finding dad. She never accepted the winter's cold. The chill that crept under the crack of our front door whined like a neglected dog, slinking meekly across the floor to lick at our ankles. Dad would roll towels into twisted green stalks to jam the cracks to stop it and tell her he wasn't made of money, drowning the furnace if she had lit it again. She would thump and rub her arms under her woolen sweater, forever too small around her huge, hunched shoulders, her head swiveling, her glances retreating to the floor. She would mutter for me to help her in the kitchen.

"Add water slowly," she would instruct as she piled her wiry blonde hair into a reasonable tangle on the top of her head, and I would push my hands into the warm dough. I always looked for faces in the sticky mass of flour, water, and oil when it was still the formless, fleshy tone of something weak and young. But it wasn't until my mother took the bowl from me, dumped the heap to the floured counter with a deft, practiced sweep, and pressed in her knuckles that any real life was massaged into the twisted little monster I had made. She would grind flax and oats with her large mortar and pestle and season the soft dough with the coarse grains.

"Fie, foe." She muttered constantly as she pulled and pushed, making something right in the confusion of dough. She rolled her words into it and filled the crust with them. When it was time to leave it alone, the bread would rise, full and round and as smooth as a satisfied belly. While it baked, I was allowed to select and crack the cold, golden eggs from the refrigerator and paint their sticky insides across the crust until it glistened.

***

"Mr. Jackson has the towering temper," my mother would say of my father as she put me to bed. This only happened on the nights they had been fighting loud enough for me to hear. She would always smile conspiratorially then, minute lines crimping the edges of her tiny eyes, her broad plain face made momentarily pretty. "But he is small man. We are giants, and we overcome."

She would sing me a song in words she wouldn't teach me, her large hands raised slightly before her, one in front of the other, as she picked at an instrument that was not there, playing me music I could not hear. She would tell me old stories filled with castles, monsters, and a twisting green tree that scratched the sky. She told me how she used to climb trees high enough to kick the clouds. I found her stories hard to believe, and she would laugh from the belly when I politely called her a liar. I would snack on a piece of the bread we had made, warmed and spread with cinnamon and butter, as I listened. When I slept, I would dream about the sky.

She would say nothing the nights he came home late slamming doors, reeking and shouting. She would lock my door and crawl into my bed, stroking my hair as she stared up at the ceiling.

***

My mother was the tallest woman I ever knew, and I dreaded the thought of ever looking (*ugly*) like her although I suspected one day I would. Her hands were not like those of the other mothers' who dropped their children off at school on those muddy mornings in spring—pretty, slim, painted. The hand that held mine was larger than most men's, with calloused fingers, and thick wrists. Her face was flat, her hair was the yellow of mown grass left to wither on a lawn, and her cheeks were ruddy red, as if forever burned in a strong wind. Her feet were gigantic, and she seemed to shake the ground as she walked me down the cracked sidewalk. Stomp. Stomp. Stomp. I noticed (*her shoes like tires*), the other children noticed (*the way she never kissed me goodbye*), and their mothers did too (*the way they smiled at me and flicked their eyes at her*). But she did not notice; her thoughts were always somewhere else. Her dreaming gave her a vacant look, her dull eyes becoming even more bovine and slow. I would have to pull her hand to make her stop.

"Huh?"

"We're passing my school." I'd drop her hand as soon as she'd loosen her unknowingly iron grip.

"Sorry," she'd say. "Head was in clouds." She'd smile her monstrous smile, showing her pebble-string of teeth, like we were sharing secrets.

Sometimes I hated her.

***

I never learned where my parents met or when they married. I suspected at one time they must have been happy, never suspecting how it would end. I wanted to think it wasn't just madness that brought them together—although some days, listening to my mother's mutterings (*fiefoefum*) and my father's sullen, sodden rants, I wondered if that was what pulled them apart.

***

She was always careful when she searched around our home, always with backward glances, like she did not have a right to be in her own house. When she caught me watching her, a thin, almost canine smile would split across her moon face like a dull mask of innocence. I would look away, strangely ashamed. She was unable to be quiet, so she would wait until the house was empty before pulling drawers, tapping walls, or digging in the backyard.

"I will find; they are mine. They are mine," she would softly chant, her nails full of earth, her hair sticking to her narrow forehead.

By the time he got home for supper, not a speck of dust would be out of place. If it was, I would walk into the field until I was surrounded by the herd, and I couldn't hear anything but the lowing of the cattle.

I would wait, and he would come to find me.

"That woman lives in her own world." He would give me an Oreo. "See what she made me do, kiddo?"

I would watch the herd and eat my cookie.

***

Dense clusters of trees bordered the fields. They were thick and wild, wasted fingerlike branches tangling on the floor. In their shadows, bleached patches of snow could survive well into the spring, perhaps into the summer. In a grove of thin maples, I climbed as high as I could one day and swinging from a branch remembered my mother's stories. I felt a surge of guilt for bringing them out here without her. I hurried to climb down.

It was below that I found the cow bones. They had been shot by my father's father, the cows too sick or old to be of any use. I began to carefully arrange the bones of one, so it appeared as if it had simply lain down on its side one afternoon, as a skeleton, and failed to rise ever again. Dad found me soon. He told me the names of the bones as I piled the spares into stacks. I never thought to question his knowledge—we were in the fields, the home of all his stories.

He picked up a rib, his shaking hands brushing away the loose moss.

"This is a bone orchard," he mused. I imagined rattling branches of ribs on tall trunks of vertebrae where daisies and yellow flowers bloomed at the skeletal roots. He took his large silver flask from his pocket, fumbled the cap off, tremors in his fingers, and finished it as I proudly recited the names back. I smiled when I thought he was smiling at me.

I told my mother about the place later.

"Oh," she told the laundry she folded. "That is nice." She then continued muttering like I had not said a word. I wished I had not.

Dad and I took a skull from the orchard as a memento one day, pairing two random jaws that seemed to fit enough to complete the grin. I shielded it from the black, watery eyes of the cattle; I did not feel like a thief, but I thought it was better that they did not know.

Back home dad told me to put the skull in his shed; he'd find something to mount it on later. I stared at him for a moment and then carried it in both hands, my thumbs looped into the musty eye sockets, and delivered it to the work shed. I unlatched the door and bummed my way inside. A bag of old lime fertilizer stooped in the corner, spilling, and old gardening tools rusted on bent nails on the walls. On the small splintering table rich with the skunky hum of old oil was a birdhouse I had made (*broken, waiting almost two years to be mended*) and his dusty axe. I put the skull on the table and moved the axe to the floor. That was the last time I saw my birdhouse, the skull, or the axe.

***

The herd got smaller every month after that. Dad was away more often, and their fighting grew more frequent. I couldn't hide in the herd like I used to, so I would stay in my room and play my music loud.

He would call her a troll. She would shout words I couldn't understand. He would say he was leaving, but he never did. There were cold nights (*the nights he was home*), and warm nights (*the nights he didn't come back until the morning*) when she would stoke the furnace. He stopped going back to the fields or checking on the cattle, but I no longer would have wanted to join him if he had. I didn't stop hating her the night he broke her nose, but I thought I loved her more because of the way she walked to the bathroom and calmly reset it with a cracked pop. When he left, she came out with a bandage between her eyes, and we made bread. She didn't instruct me anymore, and we worked together in silence—except for her muttering. She ground the grains, and punched the loaves. Fie. Foe.

***

How much time went by before it happened? I do not remember. I did not know that there was something to anticipate back then. I remember that the day that Chris Hemford kissed me was the day my mother came home from the hospital. I remember it that way, not the other way around: that Chris Hemford in his tight black jeans kissed me as we walked home, near the gas station where the street ended. That I stood on my toes for our kiss, and at home she was in the kitchen like an afterthought. It's what mattered more, at the time.

"Who drove you home?" I asked. I got a glass from the cupboard and filled it with water from the tap before I took my backpack off. I had driven her there.

"Who is the boy?" she asked, not looking up from the dish she washed. Both of her eyes looked like they had been blotted with purple bingo dabbers. I looked out the window and could still see Chris walking down the street. She had seen. "He is good boy?"

My head turned sharply. "Don't tell dad."

The dishcloth stopped squeaking around the plate she was washing, and at last she looked at me. "He saw." She wrapped her huge, wet hand around my fingers, smiled, and for an instant I thought I would cry. But then she let go and went back to work.

"Do not fear small man," she said.

It was that night, I think, that she came to my room to tell me a story. She looked too happy for me to tell her I was too old for stories and to be tucked in, and I was too consumed by what would happen when dad came home to ask her to leave. She told me one of her Old Country stories again, a story about the sky.

"Once there was great king," she said. Her accent was always soft but somehow severe; like snow pushing through pine boughs. "Who was murdered by thief. The king had been very happy. His kingdom, happy. His queen, happy. There was plenty food. The queen had a golden eagle. Every morning it would lay a golden egg, and this egg would crack every evening, releasing not just egg but a great feast. And the people were content.

"There was endless gold from purse the king wore. Every morning he would throw gold, and every day city sparkled when great sun reached over clouds and touched the shining streets. And the people were happy.

"There was such music. The queen's music box, made of silver starlight, played as moon rose and every night, dancing. And the people were merry." She paused. "But the thief took all these, one by one, laughing as he ran. King pursued, and he fell.

"With no eagle there was hunger. With gold vanished, the sun no longer shone through streets, and there was darkness. As the kingdom starved, queen's heart broke, and she lost her mind. Only music now was crying of the city. Like wolves, they mourned."

She held my chin then, softly in the cradle of her hand. "But King's daughter said, 'We are giants. I do not fear dark. I will make it right.'"

She smiled then and produced a plastic shopping bag. From the bag she withdrew an old metal box. At one time it would have been silver, but it had long ago tarnished a mottled green-grey. It flaked with dirt as she ran her thumb along the carvings and creaked when she pushed open the clasp. As she eased open the lid, a small dancer holding a harp tilted upright. She smiled as she wound the key in the back and placed it on my dresser. The small dancer began to turn, and arthritically the box plucked out a melody that was at first sore but soon turned sweet.

I lay back and listened, slept and dreamed of a twisting, green tree that scratched heaven. The branches boomed like a slammed door against the sky. The wind howled around the branches, screamed and fought. The fighting wind ended sharply, decisively. I thought that I woke once, from noises from the furnace room; heavy, wet, chopping. But it was the giant tree and a laughing man with an axe.

It was uncommonly warm in my room that night, and I woke early to the dim grey light of dawn. Later, I could not tell if I had seen her from my window, walking into the fields, covered in dust.

***

When I climbed out of bed, the whole house was warm; it was the first time I had ever known it to be so comfortable. As I walked into the hot kitchen, my feet sticking slightly to the linoleum floor, my mother looked up from her mortar and pestle. She wore the same clothes from the day before. There was bread already rising in the oven. I made myself breakfast, got dressed, and walked to school.

When I got home that afternoon, the music box, a small pouch, and six fresh loaves waited on the table. My mother sat next to them all. I removed my coat and shoes and sat down as she picked up the breadknife. I told her I wanted to go for a walk in the fields.

She carved the heel slowly off the pale bread. "Don't," she suggested.

I told her I wanted to go to the old bone orchard.

She set down her knife and took me gently by the hand. Then she got up to retrieve a plate from the cupboard and the butter and the cinnamon from the counter. She set it all down in front of me and began to cut herself another slice.

"Don't."

I didn't. She wound up the music box, and I used extra cinnamon. The small white brittle bits, too unground to chew, we lightly spat out onto the cutting board.

***

A year after the missing person report had been filed, my mother sold what remained of the farm to the first offer and we left for a small apartment across town. The fields had become wild long ago without the right care, anyway. The trees crouched over their old borders. The little maples grew broad and strong, concealing the bone orchard. The mournful singing of coyotes behind the dark branches strengthened a little more every night. The morning after I turned nineteen, I woke up and found that she had gone. She had taken the rusted music box with her but left me a note, an old leather pouch, and a cold chicken sandwich.

***

I returned the other day and saw that the herd had also vanished. The vast fields of my childhood were occupied now by a sensible pair of mares, their jumps dotting the field with broken precision. The bass rumble was gone, and the mares cared nothing for patience. Years of storms, of ice and rain, had thrashed against the maple bows; the twisted grey twigs, covered in moss and rot, had slowly hidden the bone orchard. I couldn't find it, although I tried.

I found a tree near where it had been. It towered over all the others and rattled in the wind. I was not young anymore but not so old that these steady limbs were off-bounds to me. I climbed it as high as I could. Cradled in the branches, above the field and beneath the stars. Halfway to home, I watched the firmament until it was an inky blue. The clouds of the day had not yet fled, and they piled before the moon and shone as though the light was their own, like dark castles in the sky.

WHEN YOU REACH THE LIGHTHOUSE

You do not arrive in Pendle Bay; the turnoff is too difficult to see. And when you don't arrive, the first motel on your left will not be The Blue Moon and Family Restaurant; four cars parked out front. Having not come this way, you would not stop your car, idle as the static of mid-summer rain touches your windshield, windshield wipers thumping, and then kill the engine.

But let's say that you were doing something foolish, or had done something foolish, and were tired of checking your rear-view mirror. Let's say that you hadn't meant to take the exit into the tall dark pines but couldn't turn around either. Your GPS had died; you were lost but wouldn't admit it. And although you thought the next exit would lead you back to Highway 1, after an exhausted half-hour, the green flash of a deer's eyes filling your headlights startled you awake enough to swerve, skidding, screaming tires kicking up gravel—and halting beneath the welcome sign to Pendle Bay.

Let's say you made a mistake, but it wasn't your first one today, so you went into town.

You get out of your car at the Blue Moon motel. It's late, but the attached family restaurant is still open. A neon blue "24h" buzzes next to a sleepy moon in a nightcap. The moment you open the restaurant's door, the oily scent of French fries hits you and you realize you haven't eaten since last night and are starving.

You slip into the two-seater under the blank TV in the back corner. The waitress asks if you want it turned on before she even says hello.

"Game's on," she says. You smile and say no, thank you.

You've always been polite.

The late-night special is chicken fingers and Caesar salad; you order the club sandwich on whole wheat and a glass of water. When the waitress returns with the food ten minutes later, you ask if the motel office is still open.

"No, but I handle the midnight check-ins. If you're staying in town for a while," she goes on, "you might check out the lighthouse. It's a historical site. If you like those things."

You do like those things, you tell her, but you are not staying. You thank her for the information, anyway, and she smiles. You can tell it's a rare thing that smile and you've made a good impression.

Strangers always take to you.

You're half finished your sandwich (picking out the tomatoes, you always forget to ask to hold the tomato) when she returns with a room key.

"Number eleven. I'll just add it to the bill."

You pay cash and move your vehicle across the small parking lot so that the trunk of your car and the doorknob are within reaching distance. Inside, the room is clean but tight. The bed looks like it was made up years ago. The curtains are already drawn. You unzip your jeans, letting them drop and puddle around your ankles, and step free. You use a towel from the bathroom to cover the mirror over the dresser. This task complete, you peel back the top sheet and crawl into bed. You are so, so tired.

That night, it is standing in front of the restaurant.

The morning is cold. You wake up shivering under the thin blanket and fight the urge to get up and check out the window, to check the restaurant and the car. It is still dark outside. You win this battle of wills until the world is just grey enough to call dawn.

When you open the door, one of the 1's of the eleven pops its top nail and swings down, now less a railroad track and more a broken road. Your keys are laced tight between your fingers as you peer around the door, to the trunk of your car.

By the corners of your vision, you catch two things. First, a police cruiser sailing quietly down the only road to town. Second, the restaurant is dark.

You pull your eyes away from your trunk to look. The twenty-four-hour sign is still flickering, and the front door is open a crack, but the place looks stuffed with grey.

It's time to move on.

You swiftly but judiciously strip the bed, bundling the pillowcases and sheets into a neat parcel, careful not to touch anything you will not remember to wipe. Wrapping your hand in your sleeve, you wipe down the doorknob—the only hard thing you touched—and leave the key (also wiped) in the door for housekeeping to find. As a man exits room nine, you walk, *walk*, to the passenger's side of your car and deposit the bundle of sheets to the vacuumed floor. He notices nothing. Then you walk around the front of your car, not looking at the silent restaurant, get behind the wheel, and pull smoothly out of your space.

At the lip of the avenue, you come to a complete stop. You mean to turn right and back towards the highway, but there you freeze. The police car is stopped on the side of the road. He is talking to a woman walking her dog. They chat like old friends, and you briefly wonder how small this town is. When the cop looks forward, you briefly make eye contact, and you crank your wheel left like you always meant to go into town.

The town opens to an avenue that takes you past large oak and elm trees—you haven't seen elms since you were a kid, not since disease took them all, but here they are untouched. Houses large and small line the way, all heritage, all colourful, on a spectrum from adorable to grand. A group of kids walking in the middle of the road nonchalantly clump to the gravel edge without looking around as your car approaches, and then flood the road once more as you pass. You watch them in your rear-view mirror; they don't notice you at all.

You reach the end of the town sooner than you expect. When the center avenue ends suddenly in an unimpressive community college, you turn right, down to the next main drag, the aptly named Bay Street. You roll your window down as you continue around the shoreline and breathe deep of the salt air. In less than a minute, the road begins to curve, looping back around. The town is peninsular, you realize, and having reached its terminating point it is firing you right back out the way you came. You still want the salt air to wake you. When you stop your car at the point of the peninsula, pulling into a small grassy parking lot, you see that you've stopped at the lighthouse after all.

The lighthouse stands out on an old granite breaker some distance into the cold water, accessible by a worn path. There is a plaque near the rocky footpath leading down to the beach, but a quick glance reveals that it is dedicated to some small island out in the bay, not the building. It's a nice day, beautiful in fact, but there is not a soul around. The tide is very low, and the not unpleasant scent of blackening rockweed fills your nose. The wind moves the grass and your hair.

It's very peaceful here.

The slosh and crash of the waves, the distant chuckle of a seagull, the hush of the wind itself all come to you like an afterthought. It's only after you've been sitting on the hood of your car, letting the sun warm your face for ten minutes that you realize that this is the first time you've just been still, have felt relaxed in ... you have no idea.

"It stays here," you say. And you know, this time, there's truth in those words.

A car sails down the quiet road and disappears around the peninsula as you make your way to the trunk. You stand before it, listening in a way you were not listening to the wind or the gulls or the waves. At last, you fit the key in the lock and pop the trunk open.

The body is still curled around the spare tire. The skin looks a little paler, a little greyer, but other than that there are no remarkable changes. The eyes are closed. You check the bonds on the wrists and then the ankles. It could not have gone to the restaurant last night. It was a dream.

You realize you are waiting for something to happen, for the eyes to suddenly open—though you've never seen that happen before. But to be sure you won't, you begin to close the trunk. You hate to look at it. It is the face, after all, that is the problem, that brought about this situation.

It's your face.

The person in the trunk is your identical in every way. Line for line; creases by crease. Even the small mole behind the left ear is your own. You don't have to wonder what your mother would say, at least not about the most crucial point. You already asked her in a panicked phone call placed from some small drug store miles back, and she confirmed what you already knew: You never had a twin.

"Nice day."

You slam the trunk a little too fast and place a hand on your chest as you spin around, timing a big alarmed-and-then-relieved smile as you spot the woman walking towards you.

"You startled me." You start to chuckle, and then smile down at the water. "Yes, it is."

"You're here for the lighthouse?" the woman asks. Her mouth stays open in a not unfriendly grimace as she squints against the sun. She's short and heavy-set, light brown hair back in a ponytail, bangs fluttering in the breeze. She looked your mother's age on first glance but looking again you see she can't be far into her forties. She's flexing a set of keys in her hand. You stuff your hands innocently into your pockets.

"A friend recommended I give it a look."

"I can give you a quick tour, if you like. We're not quite open for the season yet, but I'm going up anyway."

You almost tell her you have to be going—but think better of it. You should familiarize yourself with this route. A beach can be tricky at night.

"Hey, that would be great."

"Okee," she says, and starts walking. "Follow me."

As you pass through the tall grass and down the path, she introduces herself as Cathy and without losing a breath starts the beat of what would be the tour for the usual summer crowd; she's obviously done this for a few seasons. She recounts the history of the lighthouse, and the ships that once came by. As you arrive under the structure itself, she elucidates on the architecture and the architect behind it. An ambitious young man by the name of Malcolm who made his fortune and after a series of spectacularly bad investments lost it all within the span of five years back at the turn of the twentieth century. She points to a dark cast on the rocks beneath your feet.

"We call that Malcolm's Line," she tells you. "After bankruptcy, he came back here, his first and most lasting project, but his least personal favourite. He took the stairs going up ... but not coming down." She grins a little as you stare at the dark patch, wrinkling her nose. "It's actually just the high tide line. That, combined with the shade of the lighthouse, has just darkened the spot more than the rest. But it's a good story, right?"

"So, the architect didn't jump from his lighthouse?"

"No, that he did. But people don't stain like that, do they. Some say the walk is haunted," she adds, brightly. "That on clear nights, a distraught man can be seen walking up to the lighthouse. So, maybe he left a stain after all." She sniffs and sounds a trifle offended. "I've never seen him."

"You've worked here long?"

She rattles the keys out of her pocket. "Uh-huh," she says, and fits the right key in the lock, opening the door in the same twist. "Lived right down the street all my life, too. Growing up, I always said I'd leave and never come back. So, did all the people I went to school with, for that matter. Must be only about ten percent that actually followed through. Most either stay or leave and come right back after they've had a taste of the world."

"Why's that, you think?"

She looks around and up at you like she can't decide if that was a joke. "It's a good town," she says. "Beautiful. Safe. You know your neighbours and they know you."

"Because they never leave."

"Well, yeah," she says with a little laugh, like you finally get it. "Not many places can say that anymore. Believe me, I did leave for a year of school and ... it never felt right. You smell that ocean air?" She waits. You sniff and she shakes her head thoughtfully. "It gets into you. And, I think, you get into it. No matter where you are, you know that there is a piece of you waiting somewhere else and you oughtta be there, too. Anyway, this is the lower level." And abruptly she's back in tour guide mode.

It is a good tour, and the history is interesting with its share of smugglers, rum runners, and a scandalous love affair (which you can tell is her favorite tidbit). She takes you around the old lower quarters, and then up to the light (which still smells of kerosene even fifty years out of use). From the higher vantage, she points out long-vanished shipping routes, invisible lines in the dark cold bay. You stare out at the water and when Cathy has finished, she asks you if you have any questions.

"I have a non-lighthouse question, if that's okay?" You approach the window overlooking the exterior walk. Your breath blooms a grey flower there and disappears. "How fast does the water come up?"

"Real quick, we've got the highest tides in the world," she says, proudly. "Semidiurnal. That means six hours in and out. It's coming in now, but by two this afternoon it'll have gone up six and a half meters—that's about twenty-one feet. You American?"

"No." You stare out at the water, carefully counting out hours in your mind. You barely hear yourself saying, "Nice place for a swim."

Cathy sucks air back through her teeth. "Wouldn't recommend that. It looks calm out there, but between these tides and the way the current moves around the peninsula, you go out for a dip you'll be dragged half-way down to Cuba before you can blink. So, tuck your passport into your swimsuit." She chuckles, and then clears her throat. "There's a cove for that if you're interested on the north side of town. Although, it's a bit cold yet in the season."

You shake your head, a smile tugging at one side of your face as you turn back towards the stairs. "Nah. Don't like swimming, anyway."

"Don't like swimming!" she says, laughing again, and you guess for a woman who has lived her entire life surrounded by water this would seem pretty funny. She takes the lead on the stairs down. They're very steep, and she instructs you to take hold of the railing as you go down. You can tell she likes you. She is very nice.

***

The lighthouse is very dark now, but you won't turn on the light. No one is supposed to be here, after all. You try not to look at the thing in the corner.

When the sun set, you used the sheets from your car to bundle up the thing in the trunk (you can never quite think of it as a person) and carried it into the lighthouse. You don't like leaving it alone for too long, never sure if it will be gone. The relief you felt at seeing it was matched in equal measures with revulsion.

You then moved your car away from the lighthouse, parking a block away behind an old hatchback. The walk back to the lighthouse felt very long, cold dread soaking your neck. It had crossed your mind to just keep driving, out of town, out of province ... But the thing had to be dealt with.

It stays here.

You can't remember when you first truly saw it. To begin with, it was just out of the corner of your eye. A dark smudge, too far or too fast to see. Then you'd see it from afar, standing on the opposite street corner, in a crowd at the metro, or at the back of a line you stood in. Not every day but enough to keep you watching; never clear but enough to keep you second guessing. One night, you noticed it standing under a streetlight as you watched TV, and you realized it knew where you lived. You moved. In a week, it had found you again; waiting in the laundry room as you brought a full basket to the apartment basement. You dropped the basket and never came back.

Then it had been in your apartment.

The first time you'd stabbed it, severed one of its fingers as it fought back, it got away through the window. You didn't call the police and threw the finger in the toilet. When you saw it again, found it in the back alley behind your apartment, you saw it retained no such injury, and you knew it would keep coming back. When it saw you approaching, it tried to stop you, but you had been ready. When it stopped fighting, you had stowed it in your trunk and started driving.

***

You pass an elderly couple and a man jogging (his headphones so loud that he'll have tinnitus by the time he's forty) as you return to the lighthouse. Reaching the grassy lot, you stop abruptly. There is a new car parked there, almost identical to your own.

For a second, you think this is a new trick, that it *is* your own car back somehow, until three teenagers pile out. You can hear their ugly music briefly before they drop the engine. One is stolidly texting; the other two can't keep their hands off each other. As the couple pulls away from one another with a weirdly loud sucking-pop, you can hear make-out girl telling make-out boy she wants to break into the lighthouse. You stiffen and hide in the tall grass. The guy is less than enthusiastic about this change of plans. He says something about ghosts and the girl shrieks laughter, but she doesn't press the matter. They grab a clinking bag from the backseat, slam the door, and all three head down to the beach. You watch them slipping down the sand and rocks, disappearing around a bend of black pine trees before you step out from your hiding place and walk the path down to the lighthouse.

The sheet-wrapped bundle is still in the corner leaning against the old kitchen table. You drop the lighthouse keys next to Cathy's hand. You try to ignore the truly bizarre crook in her neck. You do feel bad about it. You feel glad there isn't any blood. You could never stomach blood, not even in movies. Her phone chimed once while you were waiting for it to get dark, the name "Barb" flashing on the screen. You used a piece of tissue from her coat pocket to turn the ringer down to vibrate only, and then ate the tissue. You've watched enough forensic analysis and true crime TV shows to know that a stupid thing like a fiber from your coat or one speck of dirt from her pocket found on the Kleenex in your pocket could nail you. You're smarter than that. To your relief, Barb never called back or showed up looking for Cathy. Barb likely figures just what Cathy had: It's a safe town.

From a porthole window, you watch the water creeping up the rocky beach, a lurking creature in its own right. The moon is bright, and the world has been transformed; all stark blacks, slick greens, and twinkling white.

"Almost there," you say to the bundle in the corner. You're talking to yourself, you realize. The perverseness of the thought sends a queasy laugh to your lips.

Your first plan had been to bring the body down to the shore when the tide was the lowest, around eight o'clock. You imagined yourself, under darkness, walking down the long, mushy expanse of the beach; little crabs clicking and scuttling, minute bubbles popping from tiny wet mouths; broken mussel shells crunching under your shoes; slippery black rockweed tangling around your ankles. You did not love this idea. But the sky was still only dusty pink by eight and thankfully, too, as it gave you more time to realize another problem: it would just come back. The tide, turning, would wash it right back onto the shore. And you cannot stay to see what would happen then. So, you came up with a new plan: you'd wait until the tide was very high.

Two hours after midnight, you unhook a coil of oily rope (dust speckled from years of decoration) from a peg by the stairs and sling it over one shoulder. You check the thing, prodding it with your toe, and then pick it up. There is still no smell. The sheet trails at your feet, and ridiculously you think of blushing brides as you carry it, maiden-style, over the threshold.

The night might have been warm, but by the water the air is chill. On the rocky sand around the shore, the water laps playfully. But out here on the granite spit each wave slaps like an open hand against the breakers, bursting into the air. The bay is not choppy, in fact it is relatively peaceful, but the sheer power of the tide as it idles is enough to make you stop and marvel. Each wave is a gulp, water dropping five feet and rushing back up, like out in the depths of the bay some great leviathan breathes from her belly. Down the water goes, devouring as it reaches for more. There is a hunger to the bay, and you feel a flicker of hope for the first time in days.

This will be enough.

You set down your burden and tie one end of the rope around your waist, the other to an iron ladder bolted to the outside of the lighthouse. Next, you set to unwrapping the thing. You try not to look at the face. After a hesitation, you cut away the wrist and ankle bonds with the Swiss army knife you keep in your back pocket – the same one you stabbed it to death with in the alley.

This isn't murder; it's not even suicide.

You remove your shoes.

The water in the tidal pools at the edge of the platform is very cold and you almost abandon the plan. Dragging the body by the armpits, you step backwards into the water just as a wave rises. You don't have to worry about wading; the wave breathes you in whole.

The tide is stronger and the current faster than you had imagined. Gulping in a lungful of salty water you feel the strong *twang* of the rope seconds after hitting the water. Surfacing, coughing, the lighthouse seems impossibly far away. You clutch the body to your chest as its face droops in the water, its hair drifting about its head like seaweed. You feel its hand brush over yours and you scream as another wave pounds over you, pushing you down. You let go.

You breach again, hacking and spitting. It's so dark. You can't feel your feet. The night and the bay are so black and so deep. The thought of what swims below nearly undoes you. Bobbing in the waves, arms treading, you look frantically around. You can't go back until you know.

Then, you spot it, the thing that is you, drifting on the outgoing tide, it's face—*your* face—turned up to the stars. You feel an icy plunge in your gut that has nothing to do with the bitter ocean.

The eyes are open.

You grab the rope, kicking with the waves as they roll in, pulling on the rope against the waves going out. You chance a look behind. The thing has rolled onto its face. Little waves crash about its legs, like it's swimming. Your bladder lets go as you scream again.

You kick harder, pull harder. The old rope slips in your brittle hands, tearing your frozen skin from your palms. You force yourself not to look back, not to think, not to image what's beneath you, behind you, or to feel a cold, soft hand wrapping around your ankle ...

Climbing back onto the rocks, gagging, water pouring from your face and clothes, it takes nearly a full minute for you to stand. Your fingers are as rigid as ice; it feels like your bones will break through your fingertips as you work to undo the knots in the tight rope. You begin to worry about hypothermia, but the thought is oddly distant, oddly quaint in its normalcy. Your throat works, swallowing involuntarily as, shivering, you untie the rope from the ladder and coil it around your leaden arm. You find your shoes. Seeing the dry sheets, you wrap yourself. They help almost not at all. You can't remember having ever been this cold.

You forget to be careful as you stagger back out to the grassy lot, and you hear a low, drunken whisper, "*Oh, shit.*"

You look up. A teenage boy stands by his open car door, a girl's sweater in one hand, a can of beer in the other. As you get closer, he closes the door and then lets out a relieved laugh.

"I thought you were, like, Malcolm's ghost," he says, coming around the car. He squints at you blearily. "You okay?"

"Fell in," you croak. The boy's face lengthens in concern and he moves towards you, dropping his beer and awkwardly holding the sweater forward like a lantern. Your hand tightens on the rope under the sheet.

***

You find the car keys in the teenager's coat. It's not real leather, but very soft and the lining is thick. You strip off your own sodden jacket and put on the boy's before the warmth leaves it. You feel a little bad, but not as bad as you did about Cathy. So, it's sort of okay.

You check out his car. Before, you thought his car looked like your car. But now you're certain. You sit in the front seat and run your hands around the steering wheel. Yes. This is your car.

The boy is still lying on the grass, your wet coat covering his head. You pop the trunk, and make a little room before depositing the sheets, rope, body, and wet coat inside. You'll dump the body near the highway as you drive west and leave this place forever. He saw you, and that's not your fault. It was just unfortunate. The coat slips off his face as you go to close the trunk and by the weak orange glow of the trunk light you see it.

Your face, your eyes.

You try—and mostly fail—to keep the scream in your chest, behind your gritted teeth, as you loop the rope around its neck and pull hard, pull with rage. You haphazardly twist the chords down the body and then carefully bind the wrists again to be sure. You bite down on your hand until you taste blood and finally you stop screaming. The tide brings things back, that's all. It's not your fault, not this time.

You put the car in neutral, push it soundlessly across the grassy lot to the road, and only there start the engine. A thump from the trunk startles you, but you tell yourself its just shifted. The knots are strong; they've always been strong enough before.

You keep glancing in the rear-view mirror as you drive back around the peninsula and out the way you came.

This time, you tell yourself, eyes flicking to the rear-view mirror, it will be different. You lick the salt and cold sweat off your upper lip.

This time.

THE QUIET YARD

It was hard to get a little peace and quiet in the city. Car horns, bus groans, construction, people. Jared thought he might kill for a little quiet.

The summer was hot, but the noise—the goddamn noise—made the heat feel like a wall. The kind of heat that beat you up. His face hung like an old boxer's. His a/c was deader than dust, the floor fan only moved the damp, warm air, and he had to keep his window open or suffocate completely. Every damn day.

The repairs on the Plateau brownstone next door were the breaking point. They had started work when the snow had melted and still, now early August, there seemed to be no end in sight: The squealing drills, incessant hammering, and stink and growl of work vans and flatbed trucks. The goons doing the work must have been going for the accumulative record of World's Longest Lunch Break. Quitting at noon, not back until evening when they'd resume drilling, hammering, pounding until after dark. No peace, no quiet—all because a bunch of hourlies couldn't keep their heads down and kept dragging out their work.

It was the hottest day of the summer. Jared attempted to fire off an email when a grotesque, jiggling scream came from below his window. It stopped abruptly—along with his floor fan as it panned to a reluctant halt. The email failed to send. His desk lamp blinked off and his laptop screen dimmed as it went to battery.

"They cut the power," Jared said with dull wonder. Some of the men next door were shouting. Rage sparked. "They turned off my freaking power. Hey!" he shouted out his window, turning in his desk chair, at the first workman he spotted. The workman slowed his run and noticed him pounding on the windowpane. The workman maintained a short, hopping run as he thumbed over his shoulder towards the worksite.

"Sorry, man. No time. There's been an accident."

"Your ass is about to have an accident," said Jared. "Where's my power?"

"They cut a live wire. Listen, I've got to clear a way for the ambulance."

"Where's my power?"

"Couldn't tell you."

"My office is closed. I've got to work from home, I need my wifi. Not everyone is hourly, you know, some of us want to make an efficient goddamn day of it!"

The workman stopped flat. Sirens sang in the distance.

"Snyder just got toasted like a pop tart," said the workman. "You got a phone? Make a hotspot, or some shit."

The workman ran off, leaving Jared stunned at his window.

But it hadn't been a bad idea.

He didn't have to stay here; he could go anywhere to work.

The park across the street was full, social distances be damned (not that he believed in that shit, anyway; bunch of bleeding hearts killing businesses, was all). Still: Kids screaming, boneheads kicking a sack around a circle, family barbeques, weed stink mingling with the greasy burger smoke. And each group believing their event needed its own personalized soundtrack blasted through cheap Bluetooth speakers. No, the park was out. He hated cafés, and the thought of working at a library next to some passed out wino made him sick.

He needed quiet.

Dead quiet.

A place occurred to him then. Jared got his laptop and grabbed his keys. His car was like an oven. He pulled away from the curb just before the ambulance could block his escape. Traffic was slow but at least the air conditioning in *here* worked. By the time he reached the cemetery, his mood had improved greatly.

It was such a clever idea he was surprised he hadn't thought of it earlier. It was those redneck-racket-maker's fault. If he'd been able to think straight, he would have. The Mount Royal Cemetery was massive; he wasn't sure just how big, but it was several hundred acres, at least. And if you factored in the adjoining Notre Dame des Neiges Cemetery, it must have encompassed most of the mountain that gave the city its namesake. There was something a little morbid, he mused as he passed under the imposing stone archways, about a city built around a mountain of the dead.

After a few turns among the old graves, Jared stopped his car under a large oak tree and got out. The change was drastic. Quiet. Real quiet. He closed his eyes and took a deep breath. Cooler, too. The shade of the big trees, the thick grass, and the thousands of shaded stones seemed to have dropped the temperature by a solid three, maybe five degrees. The air was sweet, and he took a deep, calming breath. That workman getting buzzed was the best thing to happen to him in weeks.

Light, clanging music broke his reverie, and he opened his eyes. A woman jogged by; no earphones for the mp3 player strapped to her lean bicep. As he watched her pass, he noticed a couple having a picnic in the shade of a towering lilac bush, talking, laughing. Not far from them, a family with two little kids playing tag between the older stones. Not a care in the world. He could do better than this, he thought, and got back into his car.

After a few minutes, he found a new spot up on Mausoleum Hill. From his lofty perch, he had a view of the rolling cemetery lawns. He created a hotspot, pulled back his seat from the steering wheel, and in minutes was back to work, car running, a/c blasting.

A car alarm panicked. Jared jumped and glared out his window. A large crowd of mourners were leaving a funeral just down the hill from him, making their way across one of the secluded yards. Some were digging around in the grass. Apparently, someone had lost their keys; they must have activated their car alarm trying to open the locked door. A humourless grin twitched his cheek. The scene would have been funny, all these folks in somber black crawling around the grass—if it wasn't interrupting his work. He released the parking brake and tried again.

Deeper into the cemetery he went, skirting the edges of the huge park. He drove further up the mountain, into a wooded section that seemed older, colder. The grass amongst the graves was long. No plastic flowers here; no one remembered anyone here. Jared was just about to give it up, return to Mausoleum Hill, and hope the funeral-goers had moved on when he slammed his brakes, car lurching to a halt. The dust plume settled and he spotted it again: A dirt road turn-off, so overgrown and the brush so built up that it was nearly invisible. A rotting sign, half-swallowed by the gnarled and ancient maple tree it'd been nailed to, read in faded, grey paint: "The Quiet Yard."

Below, another sign in red: *Attention au Gardien.*

Jared, from Toronto, couldn't read French. He spoke just enough to get by at his local depanneur. But he was fairly confident the second sign was a message for the gardeners—likely for them to clean up the overgrown area. It looked like they'd been neglecting this sign and their job for a long time. More lazy hourlies, he thought. Nevertheless, while it was overgrown, the road was not blocked. Jared got out of his car, cleared some of the brush away himself, and carefully drove on.

Green shadows closed around his vehicle. Golden light flickered on and off the hood, across his face. He winced as sharp branches tickled the doors—and all at once was nearly blinded by the sudden sunlight. He pressed the back of his hands to his eyes, then peered over the steering wheel at what lay before him.

It was more cemetery. But flat and mostly treeless, bigger than the other side. Something wary piqued in him. It shouldn't have been so flat, he was on the side of a mountain. He nearly turned back ... then he rolled down his window and took in the silence, the total silence, and his uneasiness evaporated. He pulled over, rolled up the window, and got out to wonder at the effect.

Taking his laptop bag, he shut his door, softly and with a sort of awed reverence. He'd have no more slammed a car door here than ripped a fart in a church. How was this possible? In a city this size, there should have at least been the groan of a plane, the distant hum of traffic. But there was nothing—apart from the wind rippling across the dry grass, and a pair of rabbit kits playing in the shadow of a tall black obelisk, emitting little squeaks as they rolled and frolicked. Pure quiet.

Still staring at the dreamily silent graveyard, Jared decided to walk.

The sky was brighter here, a hazy desert blue, so pale it was almost white. He glanced around at the graves. None of the stones had any names on them, or for that matter moss or lichens. They were all clean white. White as silence. He did not particularly like it but enjoyed the serene mystery of it.

A soft crunch.

He looked around.

A dozen rows over, an old man was moving dirt over a grave with a big, black shovel. His back was hunched, his coveralls dirty. A greasy ring of lank, grey hair protruded from the brim of a weathered brown cap shielding his face from the harsh, summer glare. Jared lifted a hand in salutation, but the old man did not see him. The old man tamped the ground with the back of his spade, and then with a slow, rolling motion, moved on, dragging the shovel behind him like a caveman dragging a club, dragging his feet as he shuffled slowly away between the headstones. On other occasions, Jared might have been critical of such a slouching, shambling gait—but he could not blame the old man today, not in this heat. He couldn't see a service truck, but he suspected the old timer hadn't walked all the way out here. He must have parked nearby, likely on a better serviced road, and Jared made a note to look for it when he was done.

A giggle surprised him, and he looked around with a start. A pair of teenagers in state of semi-undress were rolling together amongst some of the larger graves. The boy (a skinny thing in a polo shirt with buck teeth and red hair that made Jared think of the old Archie comics) looked up from the crook of his giggling girlfriend's neck and noticed Jared watching.

"Hey, man. Get a room," said the teen.

The stupidity of this comment nearly made Jared laugh, instead he opted to flip the kid the finger and went on his way. He did not see in the distance, near the obelisk and the rabbits, the old gravedigger raise his shovel high over his head, and then bring it down, over and over ...

Jared made it to a small cluster of trees, the only stand within reasonable walking distance. Leaning his back against a wide, rough trunk, enjoying the cool shade, he created a hotspot on his phone, dropped said phone into his pocket beside his car keys, cracked open his computer, and got to work. The minutes flew by. He hadn't been this relaxed, this focused, in weeks. His battery could last a full ten hours, he could finish his workday here.

Half-hour into his work, a strange sensation passed over him, like a draft crossing a room, although the air was as still and as hot as ever. He looked around the side of his tree.

The gravedigger had spotted the teens, who were now sunbathing with their shirts off. The girl was still in her bra and seemed asleep. The old man's shovel hung limply in his hand. His pink eyes were round and staring, and his stubbly jaw slack. Jared wondered if the old man hadn't gotten too much sun. Or maybe he was just surprised to see so much young flesh. The boy rolled over onto his elbows. He tipped his sunglasses to the end of his freckled nose. Archie chuckled.

"I'm not a ghost, man," he said. "We're not hurting anyone, we just wanted to get a little—"

A rusty shriek burst from the gravedigger. He raised his shovel, shaking it like a spear over his head, and then moved fast. The kid scrambled backwards, kicking the girl who sleepily grunted.

Another unearthly screech. The old man's jaw fell wide revealing a cavernous mouth and yellow teeth. The boy screamed as the shovel came down, separating the boy's head from his shoulders with one blow. Blood shot up like a fountain, splattering the girl's chest and face. She was awake now. She screamed, leapt to her feet, and turned to run. The old man swung the shovel again, its heavy iron pan connecting with the back of her head with a sound like a gunshot, cracking her skull and caving in her brains. She slumped over a grave like a bag of yard trimmings.

Jared stumbled backwards and ran, leaving his laptop, case, and everything in it. He slipped on the dry ground, tearing up fistfuls of grass as he crawled behind a headstone, face slick with sweat, sliding down low, his shoulders pressed against the warm stone, holding his mouth as he began to hyperventilate. Behind him came a series of meaty splats as the groundskeeper swung his shovel down and down and down.

At last, silence.

Crunch.

Shaking, Jared peeked around the grave.

The old man was digging two fresh holes. Jared lowered himself onto his belly and army-crawled across the dry grass, slinking between the graves, the toes of his shoes pushing into the dirt. Grass stained his Brooks Brothers shirt and pants, insects scurried across his hands and down his collar. Five rows of graves down. He kept crawling. After ten rows, he dared a look back. He was behind the gravedigger now, putting in distance. The girl's body was still twitching, the boy's head was no where to be seen. Jared hurried on.

Fifteen rows down.

I'm going to make it, Jared thought, eyes wide, forehead sweating, a manic grin spreading across his bleached teeth. *I'm going to make it!*

His phone rang.

The gravedigger's head snapped around, slack jaw swinging, pale eyes staring. He whirled, his rasping, inhuman screech shredding the air. Jared ran.

The air was so thick and hot, his chest grew tight as he pumped his legs. He could hear the gravedigger behind him, running, shrieking. Up ahead was his car. He was getting closer, close enough to see the sun-baked steering wheel, to read the licence plate. Jared tried to run faster and tripped over his own feet, arms pin-wheeling. He jumped over a headstone, stumbled, rolled his ankle. Frantically, he scrambled back to his feet, limping as he ran, the screams behind him coming faster and faster. The grave keeper was gaining ground, but his car was right there. Jared slammed into the scalding door, a lunatic cry of triumph bursting from his throat. He wrenched the handle and—it was locked. He patted down his pants and his shirt pockets, spun on the spot as sour horror bloomed all over him: He'd dropped his keys in the grass.

An ear-piercing shriek sounded directly behind him. Jared dropped to the ground, turned, and threw up his hands, pressing against his car, begging, "N-n-n-no!" the back of his neck burning on the hot metal as the screaming figure before him, silhouetted against the scorching sun, drew back its weapon and Jared screamed so loud his voice broke—

Silence was deftly restored.

The sun was setting as the workman rang the bell for a third time. It had been a long day at the hospital, but it looked like Snyder was going to be okay—a couple superficial burns on his feet and hands, and a hell of a headache, but the paramedics had arrived in time. The workman quit the bell and stepped backwards, craning his neck back to look up at the window above: A light was on. Mr. Peace-and-Quiet must have known they'd fixed the wire. The asshole just wasn't answering the door.

The workman stuck his hands in his pockets, jumped down the steps, and strapped on his backpack. He stopped short at putting in his earphones; he could hear the kids playing in the alley, a group of ladies laughing as they enjoyed a chilled rosé on a terrace, and someone plucking at a guitar on their stoop. He smiled: The beautiful chatter of Mile End. Whistling, he decided he'd take the long way home through the park, the hot summer sunset over the mountain soaking the streets in floods of violet and red and gold.

MOON ROCKS ON MARS

In the end, they wouldn't leave their kids. Minivans with stick-figure decals and aging hatchbacks would pull rumbling and rattling to the school curb every morning, the drivers—gaunt, tired, and red-eyed—waiting with hollow hope for someone to emerge. Occasionally, a child or teacher was seen by a window. Some days, there was screaming. Other days, laughter. Mostly, there was nothing to hear or see and nothing to do but wait. They slept in their cars. As dusk fell, the drivers would restart their engines or walk away and return to the night's work. No one thought about how things used to be, or about the light; not after what happened to Kate Robichaud.

For nearly a year, the remaining residents of Emmett, New Brunswick had watched the school, or they built the tower on the edge of the Rocklen farm. It went on and on, no return signal, no end in sight.

It began with the cow.

On the morning of Friday, May 30th, Noah Robichaud burst through the front door of the rented ranch house and breathlessly tried to explain to his mother what he'd seen on the bus ride home. It was the happiest Kate had seen him in months, since they'd traded their life by the shore for one in the fields. She closed her laptop to give him her full attention. The ground sample results her team had sent could wait.

"A cow! Up here." He reached over his head as high as he could. Kate nodded encouragingly, not understanding.

"There are lots of cows in the country, bub. Tall ones, too."

Noah beamed. "She was floating."

The kids had taken pictures and posted to their various social media, getting all the right reactions. Kate watched the video her son had taken five times, a hard wrinkle between her green eyes.

"What filter is this?" she asked.

"It's not a filter, it's real."

She smirked but a tight stone of uneasiness rolled around her stomach. "I'll get my coat."

There were four other cars parked haphazardly at the road's edge when Kate pulled her Rav onto the gravel shoulder. She leaned on her steering wheel as her mouth came open. Noah hurriedly began to unbuckle; Kate glided her hand over his chest. Five other parents and their kids were clustered along the cedar fence. Patty Henderson raised her hand to Kate in acknowledgment; the others gave her a cursory glance, then looked away.

Noah pointed. "See."

"Sure do." Kate put the vehicle back into drive as Noah protested. "Don't mess with it."

Online, it was seen as a clever hoax. Folks in town said it was an optical illusion, like those ships that appear to float above the horizon when the sun's right—but that was just wishful thinking. As the sun began to set and the shadows moved below her, the tall grass blowing in dreamy waves under her hooves, it could not be denied: the cow was floating.

She didn't seem to mind.

Kate's phone rang around nine o'clock the next evening. Noah was in the bath and she could hear him splashing as she answered.

"I better not find an ocean on the floor up there," she called. "Hello?"

"Kate Robichaud?"

"Yep."

"This is Bernice Rocklen."

"Oh." She knew the Rocklens. "If this is about the surveyors."

"I was just wondering if my boys are there?"

"Here?" Kate switched her phone to the other ear as she gathered Noah's discarded school supplies from the kitchen table. "Haven't seen them."

"Just, they said they were going to look at that cow with Carrie, and Carrie told her mother she was going to play with Noah. Carrie's not back yet, either."

"They probably lost track of time."

"But Noah's home, isn't he?"

Kate did not like the note of accusation. "He got back around dinner."

"Did he mention Blake and Jordan?"

"He—"

"Ask him now. Please."

The edge of panic was unmistakable. While there was no love lost between herself and Bernice Rocklen, they were both parents and she felt for her. She exhaled.

"I'll ask him." She began moving for the stairs but stopped at the first step. Noah was at the upper landing, cocooned in a fluffy beach towel. His skinny legs glistened with water, pooling on the hardwood and dripping down the stair.

"Everything okay, mom?"

"Fine, bub. It's Mrs. Rocklen. She wants to know about the twins."

Noah scrunched his lips together. "I told you, they went into the woods."

"You never said that?"

"Yes, I did," he insisted. "After the news lady left, they went to go find the sound near the light. But you said don't mess with it, so I went home."

"What news lady? What light?"

Noah sighed the biggest sigh of the world's most exasperated ten-year-old. "Mom!"

"Okay! Hey, Bernice?" Kate relayed the information while mentally racing back through the evening. Had he mentioned it? It was possible he told her while she was replying to an email, or he might have shouted it from another room and thought she heard. It was impossible to tell if it was an error of message sent or message received.

When Noah was asleep in bed, Kate checked reruns of the local news. The sinkhole on the edge of the Rocklen farm topped the bill. She muted the television until the furious faces of Bernice and Paul were passed; she'd heard every confused, angry outburst in person. The cow segment at last appeared, bundled into a one-minute clip of local interest stories. Just camera work panning over the cow, earthbound and unassuming once more; the Rocklen twins, Noah, and Carrie Martell hanging off the fence, holding out fistfuls of dry grass to the disinterested bovine.

It was the last known footage of the boys.

The police arrived at the house early the next morning to ask Noah about which way the boys and Carrie had gone.

"And you say you saw headlights?"

An older female constable sat across from Noah as he ate his French toast.

"No, not headlights," said Noah. "Just a light."

"A flashlight?" said the constable. "Or more like a fire?" Noah considered this.

"Like a fridge door. But big," he said. "Up in the trees."

No one took the description to heart. A search party was called. Kate dropped Noah off at the movie night being held at the elementary school and joined the rest of the town scouring the wet fields and the dense trees near where the Rocklen boys and Carrie were last seen. The adults moved out in wide fans. Scattered calls were heard from near and far. Kate found herself moving deeper and deeper into the woods.

"Is it even safe to be our here?"

Kate heard a young woman say this to a young man. Neither of them could have been a year out of high school. The young woman extended a leg and, flat-footed, hit the ground (tap-tap) like a nervous skater testing ice.

"Baby, it's safe."

"Don't call me baby, Warren," said the young woman. "And you don't know that. We're not far from the hole."

Kate cleared her throat. "It's safe."

The couple looked up at her.

"The Rocklen ground collapse was a gypsum deposit. Ground water from the river had worked it away, causing the sinkhole," explained Kate. "Different grounds, here."

The young couple stared.

"Are you that geologist Bernice is pissed at?" said the young woman.

"Kate Robichaud. And yeah."

"Annie MacIntyre," said the young woman, then she chuckled, embarrassed. "This might sound stupid, but I'd feel better searching with you."

"She can't see through the dirt, baby."

"Every kid is afraid of quicksand," Annie went on, ignoring Warren, "sinkholes are kind of like that, but all grown up, you know?"

Kate joined the two in their sweep.

"What makes the ground here any better?" said Warren after a while. He sounded petulant.

"Different rock," Kate said. When she saw the couple looking for elaborations, she added: "This whole region of New Brunswick is geographically significant. The only geopark of this distinction in North America. A UNESCO site, it reaches all the way down to Lancaster Falls. Precambrian fossils, lava fields. You can paddle up the river and see the collision of different continents. It's incredible," said Kate, and she could feel herself rushing, as she always did when she talked about her work. "But here in Emmet, there's a piece of something else, rocks not from any known continent. The sinkhole uncovered them. It's actually why I'm here."

"Another continent?" said Annie.

"Going theory?" Kate pointed up.

"The moon?"

"We don't know," admitted Kate. "But sort of like that."

"So, right now," Annie continued, enchanted, "we could be walking on the moon."

"Baby, it's been here, like, a billion years. That just makes it Earth."

"It can be both, Warren."

"My son would agree," said Kate. "Piece enough things together for long enough, aren't they one thing? He has a joke: What do you call a Moon rock on Mars? A rock." She chuckled duly when they did not. "Guess you've got to be in the business."

There was shouting up ahead. Cold dread stopped the search party in their tracks. Kate thought of Noah and made her way towards the discovery. At the edge of a pine clearing, she stopped. The search party gazed.

Every branch of every tree was upside-down. Every fir and pine and spruce bow tipped their pale undersides to the sky, like worshippers in a congregation, palms up to better invite the holy spirit. The smaller branches near the tops of the trees were bent at perfect ninety-degree angles like horns, or radio tower antennae.

Warren got out his phone and started recording.

Kate looked down around her feet. The grass blades were the same; the thin, zippered underside exposed to the sky. All around, the searchers were breaking formation, wandering up to the trees and pulling the branches or patting the trunks to confirm their basic reality.

Kate almost didn't notice the shadow move. Her eyes fought against seeing what they were seeing, but for a moment, one of the trees was not a tree.

She stood by the sink. Soap suds flicked across the counter as she whipped her hands out of the hot soapy water. She stared, water rolling down her wrists, at the sink full of rocks.

"Didn't you hear me?"

Kate spun around.

Noah was at the door to the kitchen.

"Why aren't you at the school?" she said, too fast. Noah looked at her curiously.

"It's Sunday."

"For the movie. You're supposed to be watching a movie with the other kids."

"That was yesterday, mom."

A cold sweat raised on the back of her neck and upper lip. She leaned on the sink to steady herself. Noah took a step out of the room and repeated, quietly, what he had been trying to tell her.

"Carrie's back."

The girl had been found walking up Hampton Road towards the school. A man on his way to the pulp mill had spotted her and pulled over his truck. He let her sit on the front seat and drink from his thermos of cocoa while he called the police. He waited by the tailgate for the officers to arrive, explaining later, "I didn't know if it was catching."

Somehow, word got around almost before the girl had arrived at the clinic in town: Her skin, from the top of her head to the bottoms of her feet, was covered in yellow tattoos. At least they looked like tattoos. Long lines as indelible as freckles but somehow done without scaring or bleeding. The doctor who examined Carrie wondered if they were not done with marker or stain, but no amount of washing would remove them. The lines were long, repeating, and geometric, done with a precision and extent that was not possibly self-inflicted. When asked how she had acquired them, Carrie said nothing. When asked where she had been, she said, "Right here," always followed by, "I want to go to school."

She said nothing about the Rocklen twins.

At last, she was sent home with her mother and father. She was not at school the next day, or the day after that. Noah's class made "Get Well" and "See You Soon!" cards for her in art class.

The volunteer search continued for the boys. Kate said nothing to the other searchers about her lost time, but as she looked about some of their faces, drawn and nervous in more than just concern for the boys, she wondered if she were alone. She saw Annie and Warren. Was it just her imagination that they avoided her eyes, turned their backs on her when she raised a hand in salutation?

She moved with the volunteers through the fields and back towards the woods. Kate's legs felt hollow as they approached the pine clearing. The air felt thin and warm, membranous, as though every step was through something she could not quite feel. Someone nearby was speaking lowly, rapidly. Kate looked around. Patty Henderson had her head down as she trudged sluggishly ahead. Kate thought at first she might be praying, but as she drew nearer the words became clearer. Patty ran her fingers up and down her arms, with her nails tracing lines up her neck, under her shirt, hard enough to leave thin, white scratches.

"Plans, all plans. We're all plans."

Patty's hair was pulled into a wiry ponytail, her windbreaker was dirty. The woman looked ten years older in just a matter of days.

"Are you okay?" Kate said, at last. "If you want to head back, if it's too much, I'll go with you."

Patty looked up at her, her eyes red-rimmed and sleepless.

"We are going back," she said.

All at once, Kate remembered that Patty was a nurse. She would have been at the clinic when Carrie came in.

"Do they need you at work?"

A grin split Patty's face. Her skin bunched in thin wrinkles about worn eyes as she turned her head from side to side, grinning but no longer looking at Kate, no longer looking anywhere.

"They need our work here."

People walked by them in groups of two and three. In their hands, they carried sticks, tools, spools of wire. She saw a man dragging a park bench, his red face a mess of sweat, another rolled a spare tire. As she watched, Paul Rocklen hauled at a pine branch with all his might, his hands raw and bleeding as he tried to rip it from a tree young, living tree. Kate looked down. In her hands were a set of stones. Kate looked up as a long, sinuous leg stepped from the trees.

She was in her own bed.

The wooden floor thumped hard against her shoulder as in her haste to rise she fell. She got stiffly got to her feet. Every muscle ached; every joint felt packed with cement. Her nails were cracked and black with mud, her sneakers were wet, and her sheets were covered with pine needles, dirt, and grass. She was still in her clothing. The light outside was bleary and blue; birds were singing.

"Noah?"

Her voice was hoarse. When had she last had something to drink? She staggered to her bathroom and sucked several, metallic-tasting mouthfuls of water from the faucet. She wiped her mouth.

"Noah?"

Better. She searched the house, turning on lights, until she found him. He was getting his sneakers on. The stink of burnt toast hung about the living room. In the kitchen, bread toppled from a bag, jars of peanut butter and jam were open, knives stuck to the counter.

"Hey," she said, not meaning to play it too cool in her efforts to play it calm. Her heart raced. "You got yourself up."

"And got dinner." He stayed focused on his shoelaces. "You were out really late."

Images came back to her. Long lines of people, raw material in hand, streaming through the woods like carpenter ants, single-minded in their intent, eyes skyward.

They had found the boys.

Kate almost didn't make it to the bathroom. The tap water was all that came up. When she had washed her mouth, she grabbed a bag from her closet.

"We can't go," Noah protested when she told him to get packing. "We just got here. I'm just making friends."

The school bus pulled up out front. Kate could see Carrie watching her from the front seat as Noah headed for the door. She stopped him.

"I'm going to scare you now, okay bub? Please, listen." She told him how they had found the Rocklen boys. What it had looked like. What they were now. He started to cry.

"I'm sorry," she said, holding him as he sobbed into her chest. "But I need you to be scared right now. Smart scared. Look at me."

She got down so that they were eye-to-eye. Noah hiccupped and nodded.

"There is stupid scared and there is smart scared. Stupid scared means hiding your eyes. Smart scared means keeping your scared eyes open. It's the difference between being really a coward and being really brave We've going to have to be really brave right now, okay?"

He hiccupped again. "Okay." He took a big breath. "Can we tell others?"

"Not today."

"You said don't mess with it."

"I didn't mean to. Go pack."

The bus pulled away.

Kate wrote a note, she didn't know who for. She felt very calm and figured that meant she was panicking. She splashed cold water on her face, got her bag, and met Noah at the door. He had packed too much of the wrong things. She told him he'd done a great job and got him to the door.

There was an old man sitting at the end of the driveway. Kate did not know him, but he was covered in sweat, and his hands were dirty and blistered.

"Please, get out of the way," said Kate, unlocking her car.

"They're still building," he told her. He looked at his shaking hands. "The tower. God, we built all night. You know when you take something apart to understand it? To put it right again?"

"Get out of the way," repeated Kate. "Noah, get in."

"I think that's what they're doing. But what do you do when you know the plan, have the blueprints, but the materials are alien?" the old man went on as Noah clambered into the vehicle. "You take it apart and try again and again, with everything and anything until you get a result. Take it apart, put it back. I think that's why, that's why the girl ... those boys. The boys ... how are they still alive? How is any of it alive?" His eyes started to well up.

"I'm leaving."

"I want to go home!" the old man cried. He buried his face in one arm. "I want my mother. Send a message, tell her to find me." His whole body shook, like a lost child.

Tires screamed; Kate drove over her mailbox. Noah swivelled around, kneeling on his seat, gripping his headrest, and watched the old man in the driveway until he could no longer see him.

"We should have brought him."

"Maybe next time," Kate said automatically.

They approached the school.

"Please," said Noah, and she knew he wanted to stop. "My friends."

"No," said Kate. She frowned as they approached the school. Something was wrong. The buses were lined up front but there was no one outside. Kids should have been waiting outside for the bell. A few parents milled about looking confused. One of the fathers saw Kate's SUV and, even though she was not slowing, he ran in front of her, waving his hands. She slammed the brakes; the hot stench of rubber filled the cab. She hit him. He buckled around the hood, but that was all. He held his gut as he limped to her window. She did not roll it down. He knocked on the glass.

"I can't get in," he said. He held up a sack lunch like it might explain everything. "Monica forgot her lunch; I've tried five times to drop it off. But I can't get in."

"Break the glass," Noah suggested, grabbing his mother's hand as she reached for the gearshift. "The front door."

"I can't get to it," he said. "I try and I'm here!" Kate hit the gas before he could say more. She headed for the highway. She turned on the radio. All static.

"Mom."

They were passing the cow's field. The cow was gone, so was half the cedar and electric fencing.

"Mom, slow down!"

Kate glanced up. There was something standing in the middle of the road. Thin as a needle, tall as the sky. Folds of ichor opening and closing from nothing onto nothing.

Kate sat up.

"If we finish what they want, it will all go back," Patty was telling the assembled hall. She stood at the church pulpit. Her bloodshot eyes were glassy. Her wrinkled cheeks buttressed a rictus smile of yellow teeth. Ancient at forty. "It'll all go back to normal. We just have to keep building."

Kate looked around. Half the town was crowded into the small church, and half of them had never set foot inside before. Now they knelt in the pews like the sons and daughters of the devout, wringing prayers from their hands and bowing their heads.

"Noah?" said Kate, getting to her feet.

"No children here," whispered a woman behind her. She was very drunk. "They're all at school."

"We shouldn't be afraid," implored Patty, positively beaming. "This is a plan. A beautiful plan. And we're a part of it."

"Yes," intoned half the congregation.

Kate slipped down the center aisle and did not look back.

"Where are you going?" said Annie.

"Home."

"We all want to go home," said a man.

"Then go," said Kate. Her hands were calloused, her head pounded. Something was crusted in her hair. She didn't think she could go another day like this. She flung open the doors, throwing her arm up to the sudden brightness, and saw that it was morning, but a new morning. Birds sang in the thorn bushes. No one stopped her from leaving but no one joined her either. She had no idea where her vehicle was, so she walked home. She was limping badly with blisters by the time she got there.

It took her nearly an hour to find Noah. He was hiding in her closet, hugging one of her coats.

"You left!" he shouted. His face was red and wet. "You left me there! I waited all day, all night!"

She hauled him, sobbing, out and held him for a very long time. He sat outside the curtain as she showered and would not leave her side neither as she got dressed nor when she went to the kitchen and grabbed all the junk food they had. They sat on the couch together and ate.

"The light was back," he said, scrapping the bottom of the carton of ice-cream with his spoon. He sounded relaxed, but Kate knew better. "I saw it when I was still in the car. But you went the other way, with the others."

"We'll stay right here for tonight," said Kate. "We'll figure it out."

"What's to figure out?"

"What's happening."

"We know what's happening: Something bad. You don't have to know everything about a bad thing to know it's wrong."

Noah got his phone out. Reception flickered, for just a second, and then was gone.

"We've just got to hide, ride this thing out," said Kate, but even as she spoke the words, she knew they were wrong. There was no riding this out, no pretending the problem wasn't there and waiting for better times. Whatever was here had lain with the town a long time, perhaps forever. They were more a part of the place than she was, and she could no more wait out a force like that than she could wait out a glacier.

"The light," she said at last. "You said everyone was walking away from it?"

Noah nodded. "Because it hurts. That's what a man I met walking home last night told me. That it hurts."

They stayed on the couch all day, and later fell asleep where they sat.

Kate returned home in the morning. One finger broken, a tooth missing. The coldest shower couldn't knock from her memory what had become of Annie, a piece of living material, bent backwards arms reaching for the sky like aerials. To wait longer would be madness. When evening fell, she and Noah walked out of the house together.

The light was brighter in the dark, but still much dimmer than it had been just the night before. Kate thought it would be gone entirely soon. The workers saw them come and go but did not halt their construction, stitching their tower together with whatever, whoever, they could find to fit. The Others watched them too, as tall and indifferent as thunderclouds. Kate could feel them watching, feel her own insignificance so coldly it hurt. It couldn't be this easy to leave. She would show them that they needed her, that she had a purpose here. Noah gripped her hand tighter when she began to pull away. She took at deep breath of the night air.

"We're almost back. Build back, build backwards," Patty was telling a train of builders hauling bricks, branches, library books, torn limbs. "When it's done, it'll all go back to normal. It's all a plan, a beautiful plan."

Noah gripped his mother's hand tighter, digging his little fingernails into her hand.

The light was not even far away, just on the other side of the pine clearing, and Kate could feel the warmth of it on her face as they approached. Here in the woods, it was night. But somewhere it was still the day, a place with simple earth to walk on, a simple place to start again. The heat from the light grew stronger as they got closer, as they left the builders and the moaning tower behind. All this time it had been so close to them, so close. Her eyes began to water against the heat of it, her vision shimmering. The light was growing quickly brighter. Her face and arms felt scorched, like a good sunburn after a day at the beach. She began to think of water, rolling waves, walking in the surf. No more fields and trees, no more holes. Just water and sky, the edge of the earth surrendering to the sea. Her ears began to fill with a low, steady roar, like a wave rushing back to land.

Noah said, "It hurts," from somewhere beneath the roaring sound. She couldn't see him, the light was too bright, but she could still feel his hand in hers. She scooped him into her arms. He buried his face into her neck and hair. She scrunched her eyes tight and took another step forward—buffeted back by a sudden force, staggering for a second before dragging her other foot forward. Then the other. Legs heavy. The other. Each step like dropped lead. The other. Spray like static hit her face. Cold and stinging. She stumbled, her foot not meeting ground, and for a numb second, she thought she'd fall, straight off the edge of everything—she righted herself, shifted her feet to a more stable stance and kept going. She kept her eyes closed.

The hot blinding light on her face, through her eyelids, was made black, red; electric white swirls dance behind her clenched eyes. She stumbled again, and for a second was carried back, weightless, both feet off the ground before being set down gently half a foot back. She had to look, to see where she was going. But she was scared. She didn't want to open her eyes, not before she knew she would never have to look back, that they'd never be taken back. She stumbled again as she was hit with another freezing spray.

Noah screamed, tightening his grip around her neck. She didn't want to look, but she had to. She had to be smart. Kate took at deep breath, and opened her eyes.

Tears and what felt like more than tears streamed down her illuminated face. She stared. Her mouth came open.

She could taste salt.

Was that a scream or a laugh? Warren thought, when he could think. He had seen the mother and son approach it, the light, the light of an old place that he might have once remembered. But it was too hard to go back there. He couldn't now and there was no time to think on why that was. The light was gone now, anyway, and that was days ago. Or weeks. Didn't matter. There was no time to think of fading lights, not when the ground beneath them was so unstable. They would work to fix what they had here, do as they were told. They were fixing it now. Surely it was worth fixing even if he couldn't remember quite why or what it was all like before. One day it would be better again. At the end of it all. Better like before.

GOOD TIME IN THE BAD LANDS

Marcy was sprawled across the backseat, sucking on a melting chocolate bar as Aaron screamed, "My side! My side! Stay off my side!" He shoved her thick leg with his sticky hands.

The car was hot. The a/c was dead. The parched wind pummeling the car's occupants smelled like mud. Bub, the family's unfixed golden retriever, hopped from the front seat to the backseat, drool flying off his red tongue, and barking his head off. The dog's huge tail whacked Lenora Parker, sitting in the front seat, right in the face. Dog hair stuck to her lip-gloss.

"Aaron, stop it," said the kids' mother. "You're making the dog crazy."

"It's her!"

"I'm not doing anything," said Marcy innocently, smearing her Mars bar around her mouth to lick off later. "I'm not even touching him." She pressed her toe harder on the clip of Aaron's seatbelt, clamping him tighter. Aaron shrieked.

"Would you kids shut up?" their father growled, hunched over the steering wheel, glasses slipping perilously to the tip of his nose.

"I'm just cooling off."

"My side!"

"Shut up! Shut up or I'll stop this car!" bellowed their father, Mike Parker. A vein in his temple throbbed. "Lifted Jesus on a stick, I will stop this car!"

But they knew he never would. They were making good time.

Every July, the family went to visit Mike's parents in Moose Jaw. The trip from Prince Albert never seemed long, in theory. Three hours and forty minutes, the internet would have you believe. With their iPad charged, the little monsters could even stay occupied for an hour or two. The rest of the time they whined, but even that could be broken up with a quick pit stop at a Burger King or, better still, a McDonald's. Usually the hardest part of the drive was just keeping awake; even in the daytime, the flat, unbending prairie landscape had a way of sucking you in.

It must have been a kind of madness to leave the electronics at home this time, Mike figured, as his twelve-year-old daughter kicked the back of his seat for the hundredth time. The other day he had looked at his kids (his youngest already eight) and realized he could not distinguish one single summer vacation from the other. It was all the same and mostly a blur, just like the yellow canola fields and big blue sky they passed but never really looked at every summer. Didn't they want to do something special? Marcy was already looking at boys and kissing her poster of Harry Styles before bed every night. Next year she'd be a teenager. She might get a job busing tables; she might not even want to go on family vacation anymore and would have the excuse of work to lay on him.

Then it struck him. They'd never been to the Badlands. A natural wonder practically in their backyard, and in all these years they'd never been. He warmed to the idea, already basking in the nostalgia his kids would one day pour on him like a sweet balm in his old age: stories about the great time they had that one year, that last year before the real world came flooding in and swept them away into the lifelong routines of work and responsibility.

He decided they would leave extra early, see the sights at Big Muddy, and then spend a night in a motel. Len had protested; if they were going to stay somewhere, it should be a hotel. But he wasn't made of money and he was already burning the extra gas to make this trip special.

He told the kids not to pack their electronics, they were going to have good, old-fashioned fun.

The protests had been swift and severe.

"Nothing old-fashioned is good," insisted Marcy. "If it were good, it would be the now-fashioned."

"We're going to see the sights, Marce," said Mike. "Take it in. No filters."

"That's not fair! Lots of grass, old rocks, and road. Big whoop."

"If you paid attention, you might find it's a very nice whoop," said Mike. "You'll look back on these trips one day. Best days of your life."

"Kill me now," said Marcy, flopping back onto her bed.

Aaron took it a little better, but his eyes teared up when he was told he couldn't bring the family laptop to watch movies, either.

"I'll be so bored," he said, turning on the waterworks. Silent tears slipped down his ruddy cheeks. "And so will Marcy."

"Are you crying?" said Mike, not sure if it was good parenting to laugh at his kid. But he was so tired, had been for twelve years. Confused laughter was forever on a knife's edge with a parent.

"I don't want to go to the Bad Man's, I just want to go to grandma's."

"We're still going to grandma's, just after the Bad*lands*"

Aaron tipped his head back like Charlie Brown and started to howl, revving up to a good bawl. Mike backed out of the room and shut the door.

They were nearing Moose Jaw. Soon they would be in unfamiliar territory. Mike leaned across the gearshift, one eye peeking over the grimy dashboard, and slapped the glove compartment until it flopped open.

"Hey, honey. Dig out the map and get me some directions, will ya?"

"I can't. We left our phones," moaned Len, head back and eyes closed as she fanned her face with an expired Subway coupon book.

"Paper maps, honey, we have paper maps."

With one eye over the dash and one hand steady on the wheel, Mike shuffled through old take-out napkins, a waterlogged car manual, and a lifetime worth of dead air fresheners. His hand landed on a crusty sheaf of pages torn from an atlas found at a yard sale years ago. He tossed the papers to Len's lap and sat back up. The blood rushing to his head made him see silver spots.

Len sipped from the jumbo Gatorade bottle she'd had safely nestled between her knees. It wasn't Gatorade. Without opening her eyes, she held the pages backwards over the console. Bub, laying on the middle seat, tried to lick her wrist.

"Marce, read the maps for daddy."

"Can I have a dollar?"

"You can have a dollar."

"Five dollars."

"Marce, read the maps," said Mike, "or we give Aaron the dollar."

"I want a dollar," whined Aaron.

"You got to work for money," said Marcy, snatching the pages. "And I wouldn't hire you for a million bucks." Aaron started to cry.

"Marce," said Len. "Hire your brother."

"Five bucks."

"Five, if you hire your brother and pay him."

Marcy shoved the papers at Aaron.

"One dollar. No benefits," said Marcy and Aaron started to read the maps out loud, happy to be making a wage. Marcy lounged back again and licked her lips; there wasn't anything good you could get with four dollars.

They had to stop for gas. Aaron had gotten them turned around (somehow), but it wasn't long before he realized his mistake. Still, Mike was angry.

"We were making good time," he muttered as the kids bolted from the car, heading straight to the last unoccupied picnic table beside the gas station restaurant. They clambered on top and took turns leaping as far off as they could.

Len slipped on her sunglasses and broad hat as she cradled her bottle under one thin arm. Bub barked at them from the back seat. Len cringed at the light.

"God it's so hot. How can a place that gets so cold get so hot?" She was from Victoria. She missed the unsurprising climate.

Mike began digging through the trunk. "Place this flat, it's like a clean slate; the weather can be as extreme as it wants."

"I don't think that's right."

He found the cooler at the very back, after taking out their assorted luggage and the plastic bags for extra shoes. He handed out sandwiches at the table: peanut butter and banana for Aaron, cheese for Marcy, cucumber and ham for Len and him. They leashed Bub to the leg of the table and filled his water dish from the gallon jug they'd packed.

Mike smiled around at his family as they quietly ate their sandwiches and watched the other travelers. His heart swelled with pride. This was it. This was the stuff of memory, of Norman Rockwell, of Americana. Wrong country, but same idea: The Great Family Car Trip. He'd brought his old digital camera and now was the perfect time for a picture. He'd even print this one out, display it somewhere they would always look at it and remember the good times. He got up wordlessly (he didn't want to spook the moment) and headed back to the car.

A huge SUV had pulled up beside their car. It was dark blue and, despite the dusty summer roads, was so clean Mike could see himself in its doors like a warped mirror. Two little girls in matching unicorn t-shirts hopped out of the back doors. A young woman in cute yoga pants followed suit from the passenger seat. The girls stretched as their father opened his door. It banged into Mike's passenger-side door. The young father saw Mike, and then carefully stepped out of his car. He straightened his polo shirt as Mike stood by.

"Hey, this your car? Don't think it left a mark." He noticed there were scratches all down the doors, from mirror to taillight.

"No, I'm over ... over there." Mike pointed vaguely off across the lot. The two girls and their mother were heading to the restaurant. "Family trip?"

"We just got back from Castle Butte," said the young man, not moving from his car. He hit the key fob and his doors chirped locked.

"We're on our way there, too," said Mike, proudly. But the SUV man shook his head. He slipped on a pair of Ray-Bans and dropped his keys into the pocket of his shorts.

"Weather's supposed to change. This might be a bad time to be getting there."

"We got turned around coming down here," said Mike, as though this might help things. "Son couldn't read a map."

"From here it's a straight shot, more or less. But there's a shortcut," he added. "If you go back about five kilometers–it seems counterintuitive, I know–but in the end it'll cut off about thirty minutes of drive time."

"We know where we're going." Mike had not liked the defensive tone that had crept into his voice. Neither did the young man. He turned his back to Mike and began to walk around his vehicle.

"Just saying, the window of opportunity might be closing for today."

"We're just heading out."

"Okay." And the young father strolled off to meet his girls who were quietly waiting under the restaurant portico. Mike stood looking after him, the sun beating on his balding head.

"Let's go, let's go," he told his family, back at the picnic table. "Time's wasting."

"We just sat down," said Len.

"You can sit in the car."

The kids were chasing each other. Aaron had Bub running with him. The dog spotted a ground squirrel and bolted, jerking the boy to the ground and dragging him over the dusty grass. Aaron dropped the leash. Bub got the squirrel and bit it in half, happily flinging half away as he chomped up the butt-end and ran to Mike to show off his prize. Aaron got to his feet. He was covered from neck to knees in big, ugly grass stains. He began to scream. Marcy tackled the dog, shouting, "I got the sonovabitch!"

"Marce!" said Len.

"He is!"

"Let's go!" shouted Mike. Half of the picnickers were watching the show now. He grabbed Bub by the collar and, hunched over, began to drag him away before he remembered the leash. "In the car, now."

Aaron cried that he hadn't eaten his apple yet.

Mike tied the dog to the table and threw half-eaten sandwiches and bent paper plates into the cooler. He dumped the rest of the water on Bub's snout to wash the squirrel off. At the car, he somehow managed to get the dog in the back and everything in the trunk in less than five minutes. The kids took another ten. Len sat in the passenger seat, her head back and eyes closed. Aaron refused to get in the car if Bub was still there, on account of him ruining his favourite Batman t-shirt.

"For Christ's sake, he's a dog! He didn't know," said Mike. "You were the one running him."

"It's completely your fault," agreed Marce.

"Marcy, get inside."

"Bub's all wet."

"Kids, get in the car. Mommy's melting!" moaned Len.

Mike saw the SUV man coming out of the restaurant. His daughters stood at his side like obedient shadows. Mike flung open the door and picked his wailing boy up by collar and waistband and tossed him inside. Marcy, with Aaron between her and the dog, jumped in after. The stench of hot rubber lay in their wake as Mike put the pedal to the metal and they fishtailed on the dusty asphalt back onto the highway.

The car was hotter than ever. The unrolled windows were no help. Aaron wouldn't stop crying. He had worked himself up and was hiccupping uncontrollably, maintaining a whine like a pierced balloon. Every time he began to calm down, Marcy would gnash her teeth at him, re-enacting Bub's exuberant kill, and get him started again. Len, unable to cope with the heat and noise, pounded back the rest of her bottle in three open-neck chugs and passed out, cheek stuck to her seatbelt, only rousing long enough to groan, "Too hot."

Mike could see thunderheads in the distance. The park would be closed off if it started to rain, and then what? Without taking his eyes off the road, he bunched the atlas pages together in his fist and thrust them at Aaron like a trash bouquet.

"Find a shortcut, Aer."

"He'll just mess it up," said Marcy.

"Daddy needs a shortcut!"

"Ten bucks."

"I'll stop this car, I swear to god!"

Marcy grabbed the pages and Mike, eyes dead ahead, was never sure if she did it on purpose. But the second she had them, Marcy let out a big, cartoonish, "Oh, no!"

The map pages fluttered around the cab like panicked birds. Before Mike could shout at her to get them back together, they were sucked out the back windows and sent tumbling in the tailwind of the car. Even Marcy looked shocked at how fast it'd happened.

Mike's stream of obscenities was incoherent. All he'd wanted was a good time, to give his kids a trip to remember. Was that too much to ask? He was sure *he'd* remember this trip; only a river of vodka could wash this one away. He took a breath. A species of laugh that was not entirely healthy escaped his lips. The kids quieted at once. In the stillness, he heard a flapping. A single page had gotten stuck to the sticky console between the seat and the cupholders. He grabbed it, his head nodding down and then up as he tried to read the topographical features and keep his eyes on the road. A horn blared as he crossed the median and he swerved out of the way.

A grin pressed his lips back. The page was more worn than the others had been, like it had come from a different atlas. But the map was just what he needed. Up ahead, there'd be a turnoff; it'd take them right to where they wanted to go. They'd make up for their pit stop and then some. Why hadn't he just looked at the maps himself from the start? Old-fashioned maps, they never let you down!

No sooner had he read the directions than did the turnoff appear. A crusty wooden signpost no higher than a mailbox with faded, white letters spelling out BAD LANDS materialized so fast he almost asked if the others saw it, too. Mike hit the brakes and cut hard to the right. The skidding car kicked up a plume of dust and rocks. The kids were thrown into one another; Bub hit the floor and yelped; Len jolted awake and grabbed her door handle, skinning her knuckles.

The new road was not as well-maintained as the main road, but it was empty. Mike could see some hills in the distance, and he laughed again. This road probably gave some of the best views. Locals probably knew all about this road but kept it to themselves.

The smile had become plastered on Mike's face. Not a single car behind them or in front; it was clear driving. Even the clouds didn't look so dark; everything was a little bit brighter. He pressed harder on the gas. Things were going to be fine.

"This doesn't look right," said Marcy after half an hour. The landscape was changing. The grass was greener and longer. The bare patches were hard and sharp, with huge juts of rock stabbing out of the ground at odd angles like stone knives. "We should turn back."

"No, Marcy," said Mike, grin fixed on his face. "We're making great time."

More rocks joined the sharp outcrops. Aaron thought they looked like the giant termite hills he'd seen on a nature show. Vines twisted up some of the rocks; flowers with huge, waxy leaves and enormous purple and yellow heads swayed between others.

"Michael," said Len softly. The sky had taken on an interesting shade of pink. Small green clouds roiled above them, rubbing across the sky like enormous snail trails. The plant life on the sides of the road began to stretch and writhe.

Aaron began to cry, "Daddy, go back!" as Marcy put on a high, mocking voice, "Go back! Whine, whine, whine. That's you. You just whine, whine, whine, whine!" she laughed, and Len began to fan herself again, "It's too hot, kids please. I can't take it."

A huge, dark shadow passed over the car. Marcy began to giggle, a weird and guttural chortling. Aaron shrieked louder, "Go back!"

The air shimmered like warped glass. A smell like burning hair began to fill the car. Aaron rolled up his window, but the others stayed open. The overgrowth in the ditches whipped lightly at the car doors and created a syncopated, metal drumming.

Something darted in front of the car. Mike hit it dead on, thumping over the body, but they'd all seen it: a ground squirrel the size of a pit bull with teeth like knitting needles jutting out of its fleshy, pink mouth. The abomination got caught up under the car, bouncing the vehicle as it pounded along. Mike swerved to shake it loose, leaving a bloody trail for fifty meters before it was dislodged. Marcy laughed and beat on the back window. Aaron's crying shrieks reached an almost soundless high.

"I can't take it," muttered Len, as the kids giggled and screamed, sinking deeper into her chair. "I can't."

The huge shadow passed by again. The whole car jolted. Mike glanced up. Massive claws punctured the roof with a crinkling grind of metal. The windshield exploded as the roof peeled back like a sardine can. The huge creature lifted upwards with two powerful beats of its leathery wings, dropping the scrap roof on the road behind them. The creature swooped low and shot past. Mike saw it had no face—just one huge, black eye.

"How does it eat!" shouted Marcy, laughing more steadily. She threw her arms around Mike's seat and chest. Her forearms appeared greenish in the light, mottled with tiny, yellow warts.

"Daddy's trying to drive," he told her. There was a great ripping sound and half his headrest was bitten off.

The giant bat reeled around, coming back.

"Make dad turn around!" Aaron screamed, beating on his mother's seat.

"I can't," Len muttered, over and over. "I can't, I can't..."

"We're almost there, Aer-bear!" Mike cheered. The wind rushed through his hair, tossed his glasses aside and out of the car. He didn't need them; he could see just fine. "Just a little further!"

The bat sailed over and, without losing a beat, grabbed Aaron. Within seconds, his screams were too distant to be heard.

"Wow!" said Mike. "Can that thing move!"

Marcy whirled around, jumped on her seat, and gibbered excitedly. She was no longer making words. Knots bulged up her spine and she dug at the seat with her clawed feet. Bub barked, scrambling to get into the front. Marcy caught the dog's tail with her teeth. Blood slashed across the seat. With a frantic, almost human yelp, the dog leapt from the moving car and bolted into the ever-growing underbrush. Marcy screeched, vaulted from the car, and gave delighted chase.

"Don't worry about the dog, honey," Mike assured Len, his grin reaching all the way to his ears. "Marce'll get him."

"I can't," Len repeated. The words were flabby and sluggish. Her lips had become an upside-down U; the skin of her face stuck to her chin and her chest, as she slowly puddled into the seat. She melted to the floor in glossy, reeking tendrils.

"That's okay, honey!" But when he looked over, she had already slipped out the crack at the bottom of her door. That was okay, too. Less weight in the car, faster on the road! Mike pressed down on the gas. The tailpipe dragged and sparked; licks of flame shot out the exhaust.

His eyes grew huge and excited as the wind whipped his hair around. Nothing like a good, old-fashioned road trip. He could see something ahead. The end of the road, maybe, or perhaps something bigger. He couldn't tell. It didn't matter.

He was making really great time.

ACKNOWLEDGMENTS

I'd like to thank my husband, John, for your endless support, encouragement, and love. And my son, to whom this book is dedicated. Thank you, sweetheart, for always reminding me to do at least one fun thing a day. And you tell the best stories already. I'm so proud.

Thank you also to Joe Sullivan of Cemetery Gates for reaching out and making this collection possible. My gratitude forever.

And to everyone who first read these stories, provided early reviews and/or blurbs, or otherwise encouraged me and my twisted little tales on. I only hope I can go on scaring you for years to come. My thanks.

Photo by Selena PB, Life by Selena 2022

Laura Keating grew up on scary stories. She lives in south shore Nova Scotia with her husband and son. To find more of her work, please visit www.lorekeating.com, or follow her on Twitter, Instagram, and TikTok @lorekeating.

Made in the USA
Middletown, DE
11 August 2024